The house they call The Corbuthut. On this page: They Call It The Council Estate

Faces at the window as a Black Maria takes the Kray twins and others from the Old Bailey to Brixton prison

Timber bitters Ashton Avenue, Bristol. On Page 5: Lorry Scatters Its Props

PAGE 2: Financial
PAGE 3: News; Mr West's Diary
PAGE 4: Women, news, TV, crossword; Miss West
PAGE 5: News
PAGE 6: Jerusalem, The Arabs And The Future
PAGE 7: News
PAGES 8 & 9: Gloucestershire Property Guide, Professional and Technical Appointments
PAGE 10: Classified News
PAGE 11: Sunshine Club, sport
PAGE 12: Sport

THE PAPER THAT FIGHTS FOR THE WEST   WEDNESDAY, MARCH 5, 1969

KRAYS GUILTY

Nine of 10 accused will be sentenced today

Western Daily Press Reporter

THE KRAY twins, Ronald and Reginald, were found guilty of murder last night, at the end of the 29-day Old Bailey trial.

After the jury returned their verdicts, Mr Justice Stevenson said sentences would be passed today.

Ronald Kray was found guilty of murdering Jack (the Hat) McVitie, and of...

Berlin link is cut two hours

Heavy guards

Meet the mayor

The bull you can lead by the nose

They call it The Council Estate

By Robert Simmons

THE COUNCIL Estate — that is the name they are giving at Bradford-on-Avon to a group of exclusive homes being built on the edge of the town.

Planner take 5

Thanks to

our team

2016

published in

the U.S

kray publishers

By Kray publishers

u.s

contents

introduction to the krays

Twin brothers **Ronald "Ronnie" Kray** (24 October 1933 – 17 March 1995) and **Reginald "Reggie" Kray** (24 October 1933 – 1 October 2000) were English gangsters who were the foremost perpetrators of organized crime in the East End of London during the 1950s and 1960s. With their gang, the Firm, the Krays were involved in armed robberies, arson, protection rackets, assaults, and the murders of Jack "the Hat" McVitie andGeorge Cornell.

As West End nightclub owners, they mixed with politicians and prominent entertainers such as Diana Dors, Frank Sinatra, and Judy Garland. The Krays were much feared within their milieu; in the 1960s, they became celebrities, even being photographed by David Bailey and interviewed on television.

They were arrested on 9 May 1968 and convicted in 1969, by the efforts of detectives led by Detective Superintendent Leonard "Nipper" Read. Both were sentenced to life imprisonment. Ronnie remained in Broadmoor Hospital until his death on 17 March 1995; Reggie was released from prison on compassionate grounds in August 2000, eight weeks before his death[5] from cancer.

Ronnie and Reggie Kray were born on 24 October 1933 in Hoxton, East London, to Charles David Kray (10 March 1907 – 8 March 1983), a scrap gold dealer, and Violet Annie Lee (5 August 1909 – 4 August 1982).

They were identical twins, Reggie being born 10 minutes before Ronnie. Their parents already had a seven-year-old son, Charles James (9 July 1927 – 4 April 2000). A sister, Violet (born 1929), died in infancy. When the twins were three years old, they contracteddiphtheria. Ronnie almost died in 1942 from a head injury suffered in a fight with Reggie.

The twins first attended Wood Close School in Brick Lane, and then Daniel Street School. In 1938, the Kray family moved from Stean Street in Hoxton, to 178 Vallance Road in Bethnal Green. At the beginning of World War II, 32-year-old Charles Kray was conscripted into the army, but he refused to go and went into hiding.

The influence of their maternal grandfather, Jimmy "Cannonball" Lee, caused the brothers to take up amateur boxing, then a popular pastime for working-class boys in the East End. Sibling rivalry spurred them on, and both achieved some success. They are said to have never lost a match before turning professional at age 19.

The Kray twins were notorious locally for their gang and its violence, and narrowly avoided being sent to prison several times. Young men were conscripted for National Service at this time, and in 1952 they were called up to serve with the Royal Fusiliers. They reported, but attempted to leave after only a few minutes. The corporal in charge tried to stop them, but Ronnie punched him in the chin, leaving him seriously injured. The Krays walked back to the East End "just in time for tea". The next morning they were arrested and turned over to the army.

While absent without leave, they assaulted a police constable who tried to arrest them. They were among the last prisoners held at the Tower of London, before being transferred to Shepton Mallet military prison in Somerset for a month, to await court-martial. They were convicted and sent to the Home Counties Brigade Depot jail in Canterbury, Kent.

Their behaviour in prison was so bad that they both received dishonourable discharges from the army. During their few weeks in prison, when their conviction was certain, they tried to dominate the exercise area outside their one-man cells. They threw tantrums, emptied their latrine bucket over a sergeant, dumped a dixie (a large food/liquid container full of hot tea on another guard, handcuffed a guard to their prison bars with a pair of stolen cuffs, and set their bedding on fire.

When they were moved to a communal cell, they assaulted their guard with a china vase and escaped. Quickly recaptured and awaiting transfer to civilian authority for crimes committed while at large, they spent their last night in Canterbury drinking cider, eating crisps, and smoking cigarillos courtesy of the young national servicemen acting as their guards

Their criminal records and dishonourable discharges ended their boxing careers, and the brothers turned to crime full-time. They bought a run-down snooker club in Bethnal Green, where they started several protection rackets. By the end of the 1950s, the Krays were working for Jay Murray from Liverpool and were involved in hijacking, armed robbery and arson, through which they acquired other clubs and properties. In 1960 Ronnie Kray was imprisoned for 18 months for running a protection racket and related threats. While he was in prison, Peter Rachman, head of a violent landlord operation, gave Reggie a nightclub called Esmeralda's Barn on the Knightsbridge end of Wilton Place next to Joan's Kitchen, a bistro. The location is where the Berkeley Hotel now stands, on the corner opposite the church.

This increased the Krays' influence in the West End, by now making them celebrities as well as criminals. They were assisted by a banker named Alan Cooper, who wanted protection from the Krays' rivals, the Richardsons, based in South London

In the 1960s, they were widely seen as prosperous and charming celebrity nightclub owners and were part of the Swinging London scene. A large part of their fame was due to their non-criminal activities as popular figures on the celebrity circuit, Barbara Windsor and singer Frank Sinatra.

being photographed by <u>David Bailey</u> on more than one occasion; and socialising with <u>lords</u>, <u>MPs</u>, socialites and show business characters including actors <u>George Raft</u>, <u>Judy Garland</u>, <u>Diana Dors</u>,

The Krays also came into the public attention when an exposé in the tabloid newspaper *Sunday Mirror* alleged that Ron had had a sexual relationship with Robert Lord Boothby, a Conservative politician. Although no names were printed, after the twins threatened the journalists involved and Boothby threatened to sue, the newspaper backed down. It sacked the editor, printed an apology and paid Boothby £40,000 in an out-of-court settlement. Because of this, other newspapers were unwilling to expose the Krays' connections and criminal activities. Much later, Channel 4 established the truth of the allegations and released a documentary on the subject, *The Gangster and the Pervert Peer* (2009).

The police investigated the Krays on several occasions, but the brothers' reputation for violence made witnesses afraid to testify. There was also a problem for both main political parties. The Conservative Party was unwilling to press the police to end the Krays' power for fear the Boothby connection would again be publicised, and the Labour Party's MP Tom Driberg was also rumoured to have had a relationship with Ron Kray

On 12 December 1966 the Krays helped Frank Mitchell, "the Mad Axeman", to escape from Dartmoor Prison. Ronnie had befriended Mitchell while they served time together in Wandsworth prison. Mitchell felt the authorities should review his case for parole, so Ronnie felt he would be doing him a favour by getting him out of Dartmoor, highlighting his case in the media and forcing the authorities to act.

Once Mitchell was out of Dartmoor, the Krays held him at a friend's flat in Barking Road, East Ham. As a large man with a mental disorder, he was difficult to control. He disappeared, but the Krays were acquitted of his murder. Freddie Foreman, a former member of the Firm, claimed in his autobiography *Respect* that Mitchell was shot by him and his body disposed of at sea.

Ronnie Kray shot and killed George Cornell, an associate of the Richardsons, leaders of a rival gang, at the Blind Beggar pub in Whitechapel on 9 March 1966. Ronnie was drinking in another pub when he learned of Cornell's location. He went there with his brother's driver John Dickson and his assistant Ian Barrie but killed Cornell alone. Just before he died, Cornell remarked "Well, look who's what the cat dragged in."

There are differing motives offered for the murder

Daily Mirror

5d. Wednesday, March 5, 1969   No. 20,276

GUILTY OF MURDER

According to some sources, Ronnie killed Cornell because on Christmas 1965, during a confrontation between the Krays and the Richardson gang at the Astor Club, Cornell referred to Ronnie as a "fat poof". The confrontation resulted in a gang war, and about three months later, on 8 March 1966, Richard Hart, Ronnie's associate, was murdered at 'Mr Smith's Club' in Catford. A member of the Richardson gang "Mad" Frankie Fraser was taken to court for Hart's murder but was found not guilty. Another member of the Richardson gang, Ray "The Belgian" Cullinane testified that he saw Cornell kicking Hart. Due to intimidation, witnesses would not cooperate with the police in Hart's case, and the trial ended inconclusively without pointing to any suspect in particular

The Krays' criminal activities remained hidden behind their celebrity status and "legitimate" businesses. In October 1967, four months after the suicide of his wife Frances, Reggie was allegedly encouraged by his brother to kill Jack "the Hat" McVitie, a minor member of the Kray gang who had failed to fulfil a £1,000 contract paid to him in advance to kill Leslie Payne. McVitie was lured to a basement flat in Evering Road, Stoke Newington, on the pretence of a party. Upon entering, he saw Ronnie Kray seated in the front room. As Ronnie approached him he let loose a barrage of verbal abuse and cut him below his eye with a piece of broken glass. It is believed that an argument then broke out between the twins and McVitie. As the argument got more heated, Reggie Kray pointed a handgun at McVitie's head and pulled the trigger twice, but the gun failed to discharge. McVitie was then held in a bearhug and Reggie Kray was handed a carving knife. He stabbed McVitie in the face and stomach, driving the blade into his neck whilst twisting the knife, not stopping even as McVitie lay on the floor dying. However, it was thought that Reggie never intended to kill McVitie and he was lured to the basement flat to be put straight by the twins, not killed.

Several other members of the Firm including the Lambrianou brothers (Tony and Chris) were convicted of this. In Tony Lambrianou's biography, he claims that when Reggie was stabbing Jack, his liver came out and he had to flush it down the toilet. McVitie's body has never been recovered.

When Inspector Leonard "Nipper" Read of Scotland Yard was promoted to the Murder Squad, his first assignment was to bring down the Kray twins. It was not his first involvement with them. During the first half of 1964, Read had been investigating their activities, but publicity and official denials of allegations of Ron's relationship with Boothby made the evidence he collected useless. Read went after the twins with renewed activity in 1967, but frequently came up against the East End "wall of silence", which discouraged anyone from providing information to the police.

Nevertheless, by the end of 1967 Read had built up enough evidence against the Krays. Witness statements incriminated them, as did other evidence, but none made a convincing case on any one charge. Early in 1968 the Krays employed a man named Alan Bruce Cooper, who sent Paul Elvey to Glasgow to buy explosives for a car bomb. Elvey was the radio engineer who put Radio Sutch, later renamed Radio City, on the air in 1964. Police detained him in Scotland and he confessed to being involved in three murder attempts. The evidence was weakened by Cooper, who claimed he was an agent for the United States Treasury Department investigating links between the American Mafia and the Kray gang. The botched murders were his attempt to put the blame on the Krays. Read tried using Cooper, who was also being employed as a source by one of Read's superior officers, as a trap for the Krays, but they avoided him.

Eventually, a Scotland Yard conference decided to arrest the Krays on the evidence already collected, in the hope that other witnesses would be forthcoming once the Krays were in custody. On 8 May 1968, the Krays and 15 other members of their "firm" were arrested. Many witnesses came forward now that the Krays' reign of intimidation was over, and it was relatively easy to gain a conviction. The Krays and 14 others were convicted, with one member of the Firm being acquitted. One of the firm members who provided a lot of the information to the police was arrested yet only for a short period.

The twins' defence, under their counsel John Platts-Mills, QC, consisted of flat denials of all charges and the discrediting of witnesses by pointing out their criminal past. The judge, Mr Justice Melford Stevenson said: "In my view, society has earned a rest from your activities. Both were sentenced to life imprisonment, with a non-parole period of 30 years for the murders of Cornell and McVitie, the longest sentences ever passed at the Old Bailey (Central Criminal Court, London) for murder Their brother Charlie was imprisoned for 10 years for his part in the murders.

On 11 August 1982, under tight security, Ronnie and Reggie Kray were allowed to attend the funeral of their mother Violet, who had died of cancer the week before, but they were not allowed to attend the graveside service at Chingford Mount Cemetery in East London where their mother was interred in the Kray family plot. The service was attended by celebrities including Diana Dors and underworld figures known to the Krays. The twins did not ask to attend their father's funeral when he died in March 1983, to avoid the publicity that had surrounded their mother's funeral.

In 1985, officials at Broadmoor Hospital discovered a business card of Ron's, which prompted an investigation. It revealed the twins – incarcerated at separate institutions – plus their older brother Charlie Kray and an accomplice not in prison, were operating a "lucrative bodyguard and 'protection' business for Hollywood stars". Documents released under Freedom of Information laws revealed that officials were concerned about this operation, called Krayleigh Enterprises, but believed there was no legal basis to shut it down. Documentation of the investigation showed that Frank Sinatra hired 18 bodyguards from Krayleigh Enterprises during 1985.

Ronnie Kray was a Category A prisoner, denied almost all liberties, and not allowed to mix with other prisoners. Reggie Kray was locked up in Maidstone Prison for 8 years (Category B). In his later years, he was downgraded to Category C and transferred toWayland Prison in Norfolk

Ronnie was eventually certified insane in 1979 and lived the remainder of his life in Broadmoor Hospital in Crowthorne, Berkshire. He died on 17 March 1995 of a heart attack, aged 61, at Wexham Park Hospital in Slough, Berkshire.

During his incarceration, Reggie became a born-again Christian. After serving more than the recommended 30 years he was sentenced to in March 1969, he was freed from Wayland on 26 August 2000. He was 66, and was released on compassionate grounds for having inoperable bladder cancer. The final weeks of his life were spent with his wife Roberta, whom he had married while in Maidstone Prison in July 1997, in a suite at the Townhouse Hotel at Norwich, having left Norwich Hospital on 22 September 2000. On 1 October 2000, Reggie died in his sleep. Ten days later, he was buried beside his brother Ronnie in Chingford Mount Cemetery.

Older brother Charlie Kray was released from prison in 1975 after serving seven years, but was sentenced again in 1997 for conspiracy to smuggle cocaine in an undercover drugs sting. He died in prison of natural causes on 4 April 2000, aged 73

Ronnie was openly bisexual, evidenced by his book *My Story* and a comment to writer Robin McGibbon on *The Kray Tapes*, wherein he states: "I'm bisexual, not gay. Bisexual." He also planned on marrying a woman named Monica in the 1960s whom he had dated for nearly three years. He called her "the most beautiful woman he had ever seen." This is mentioned in Reggie's book *Born Fighter*. Also, extracts are mentioned in Ron's own book *My Story* and Kate Kray's books *Sorted*, *Murder, Madness and Marriage*, and *Free at Last*.

Ron was arrested before he had the chance to marry Monica and, even though she married Ronnie's ex-boyfriend, 59 letters sent to her between May and December 1968 when he was imprisoned show Ron still had feelings for her, and his love for her was very clear. He referred to her as "my little angel" and "my little doll". She also still had feelings for Ronnie. These letters were auctioned in 2010.

A letter, sent from prison in 1968, from Ron to his mother Violet also references Monica; "if they let me see Monica and put me with Reg, I could not ask for more." He went on to say, with spelling mistakes, "Monica is the only girl I have liked in my life. She is a luvely little person as you know. When you see her, tell her I am in luve with her more than ever." Ron subsequently married twice, wedding Elaine Mildener in 1985 at Broadmoor chapel before the couple divorced in 1989, following which he married Kate Howard, who he divorced in 1994

I'm Reggie Kray's secret daughter

WHEN THE last of the notorious Kray brothers was laid to rest he took one final secret to the grave with him. Among the thousands of mourners who gathered in London's East End to pay their last respects to Reggie Kray was the secret daughter he did not want to know. Sandra Ireson, a 42-year-old mother and gran, was born after a brief romance between Reggie and cabaret dancer Greta Harper in 1958. And she didn't discover who her real father was until 1995 following the death of Reggie's twin brother Ronnie. For the next five years she tried to forge a relationship with Britain' s best-known long-term prisoner. But only once did she manage to meet Reggie, who was jailed for life in 1969 for stabbing small-time villain Jack "The Hat" McVitie. Sandra, now 42, briefly hugged the ageing mobster after an hour-long chat inside Maidstone Prison two years before his death from bladder cancer, in October last year. But he later rejected his daughter's attempt to cement their relationship. He had been devastated by the death of his elder brother Charlie in April last year and feared upsetting his young wife Roberta, 41. But last night, speaking exclusively to the Sunday Mirror, Sandra said: "I am his daughter and I couldn't care less who knows.

"I don't feel any shame about who my real father is. It's time it was out in the open and the world knew the truth." Sandra's existence was until now, a closely-guarded secret known only to her family and a handful of Kray's close associates. She was told the truth by an aunt - years after both her mother and the man she thought was her father had died.

Reg kray here

Sandra, whose son Tim, 20, is the spitting image of the young Reggie, was stunned. But as she and half-sister Tracey, 39, absorbed the news, things began to fall into place. "All through my life I felt something was not quite right," said Sandra who lives in a detached home in King's Lynn, Norfolk with husband David, 43, and Tim. "I knew Mum and Dad worked for the twins in London in the 50s and they often talked about them. "But it was when I asked my Auntie Anne about it that she said:" There' s something you should know, Reggie is actually your father.' "Once we started thinking about it, it made a lot of other things make sense. My Nan, who was my mum's mother, always said, 'I've always treated you two girls exactly the same'. "It was said as if she should have said afterwards, 'Even though you' ve got different Dads'." Sandra, whose daughter Tammy, 21, and two-year-old grand-daughter Zilanne live near her in King's Lynn, added: "My son Tim has always asked where he got his big nose from. Now he knows. "He laughs about the fact that he's Reggie Kray's grandson." Sandra was conceived when her mother, Greta Harper, then 21, had an affair with Kray, 24 at the time. Greta was working at the RR club in London's West End as Reggie and twin Ronnie were beginning their reign of terror in underworld London.

Reggie's affair with Greta lasted on and off for around eight months after her relationship with regular lover Jimmy Steptoe hit a difficult patch. But by the time Sandra was born Kray had ended the affair and Greta was back together with Steptoe. And as the family moved to Norfolk to run a caravan park, Jimmy raised Sandra as his own. It was when Sandra finally found out the truth that she struggled to forge a relationship with the notorious gangster. She wrote to him in prison and he phoned and agreed to see her. Sandra said: "It came as a real shock. He just said,'I think you better come and see me'. He said he would send me a visiting order. Straight after he spoke to me, he posted it to me and Igot it the next day." The scrawled note, in Kray's distinctive style, reads: "Sandra, good to talk to you. You have nice soft voice. Will arrange a visit. God bless, Reg."

That one meeting with her natural father happened on October 7, 1998, when they spoke for an hour in Maidstone Prison. "When I first saw him. I remember thinking, 'Oh God he's a little old man'. I expected him to be much bigger than he was and to fill the doorway when he came in. "But he was smartly dressed in a nice shirt and trousers and his manner was nice. It was quite formal to start with. "When he first came in he shook my hand and just said, 'We better get this sorted out'. As we talked more he relaxed. He said: "I am not frightened of the truth but I have got to know that it is the truth. "He said he would leave the ball with me and told me to get back to him. "And then when he stood up to go he gave me a cuddle and a kiss on the cheek." Yet they were to have no further contact as Kray became pre-occupied with fighting drugs charges brought against his older brother, Charlie. And Sandra was left distraught by Reggie's death. She blames much of Kray's reluctance to contact her on his wife Roberta. "Once I left that prison I never heard from him again," she said. "I can only think it it because of Roberta, who is the same age as me and didn't want to know about his secret daughter. "I wrote a letter telling him he was messing up my life but even that didn't get a response."

That one meeting with her natural father happened on October 7, 1998, when they spoke for an hour in Maidstone Prison. "When I first saw him. I remember thinking, 'Oh God he's a little old man'. I expected him to be much bigger than he was and to fill the doorway when he came in. "But he was smartly dressed in a nice shirt and trousers and his manner was nice. It was quite formal to start with. "When he first came in he shook my hand and just said, 'We better get this sorted out'. As we talked more he relaxed. He said: "I am not frightened of the truth but I have got to know that it is the truth. "He said he would leave the ball with me and told me to get back to him. "And then when he stood up to go he gave me a cuddle and a kiss on the cheek." Yet they were to have no further contact as Kray became pre-occupied with fighting drugs charges brought against his older brother, Charlie. And Sandra was left distraught by Reggie's death. She blames much of Kray's reluctance to contact her on his wife Roberta. "Once I left that prison I never heard from him again," she said. "I can only think it it because of Roberta, who is the same age as me and didn't want to know about his secret daughter. "I wrote a letter telling him he was messing up my life but even that didn't get a response."

But Reggie did open his heart to close friends about the daughter he had kept secret from the world . Jan Lamb, 51, a long-term Kray associate and an ex-lover of Reggie' s, said last night: "Reggie wanted people to know about Sandra. "He feared people might use her and her family to get back at him if they knew about his daughter when he was alive. "But he wanted the world to know about her after he was gone. It was his dying wish." When Kray died of bladder cancer last October, it left Sandra frustrated over the lost relationship. "I was distraught," said Sandra,"I thought 'How dare you die before this is sorted out'. I couldn't believe it." Despite her feelings, Sandra went to his funeral. "I felt I had to, or I might regret it. "I would have liked to have known him and for him to know my kids and to have had some sort of relationship. I think it would have given him something. Sandra, whose family run a pub in King's Lynn, does not condemn her father for the way he lived his life. "Everyone is different," she said. "You have got choices in life. If you want to go the wrong way in life and can live with the consequences that's up to you. "And it was awful that they kept Reggie inside for so long. "No matter who he was, it is really bad that somebody was treated like that. "I always hoped they would let him out so that something could happen. "Reg would never have taken my Dad's place. He would have just been Reg I suppose. "But he would have been fun to have around."

Reg Kray

Krays gangster admits he dumped a body for the twins but insists they were NOT legends

For a decade the Kray twins ruled the East End with an iron fist, sipping champagne with Judy Garland and Barbara Windsor while leaving a trail of blood and broken bones in their wake.
And East End gangster Chris Lambrianou was the man forced to clean up that mess.

For a decade the Kray twins ruled the East End with an iron fist, sipping champagne with Judy Garland and Barbara Windsor while leaving a trail of blood and broken bones in their wake.
And East End gangster Chris Lambrianou was the man forced to clean up that mess.
It was a dark and dangerous job.
Lambrianou and his brother Tony were close to shooting two police officers to escape after the Krays forced them to dump the body of hitman Jack 'the Hat' McVitie in October 1967.

"The Krays have passed into folklore now," he says.
"They are an industry and everyone wants a piece of it.
"But the Krays weren't glamorous and they weren't legends. There is nothing legendary about murdering a man in front of 16 people.
"A legend is somebody who does the right things, somebody you can really look up to.
"The Krays could have been legends, they could have made a difference. But they chose a different path.

"They destroyed so many families. And I'll tell you what, they really disappointed me."
Speaking in depth about that night for the first time, Lambrianou reveals how he cleaned up the flat in Evering Road, Stoke Newington, in London after Reggie Kray stabbed McVitie in the middle of a party.
Wearing a pair of socks as gloves he mopped up McVitie's blood and poured it down the toilet.
But when he went into the bedroom to fetch a blanket to wrap the body, he found two young children asleep and realised the Krays had been babysitting for a friend when they murdered McVitie.
Lambrianou says: "What the Krays did was utter madness, murdering a man in front of 16 witnesses AND with two children asleep upstairs.

I couldn't believe even the Krays would do something like that."
The Krays lured McVitie to Evering Road to confront him about a hit he had failed to carry out.

Lambrianou saw Reggie pull an gun on McVitie. It was not loaded, a "frightener" the Krays often used to intimidate people.

Nonetheless Lambrianou decided to leave before things became any more heated.

When he returned several hours later looking for Tony he was confronted with a scene from a horror film.

someone had pressed a knife into Reggie's hand. High on a cocktail of drink and drugs and egged on by his brother Ronnie, he leapt at McVitie stabbing him repeatedly in the face and chest. The Krays then fled.

Lambrianou says: "I went downstairs and saw Jack the Hat lying there. There was blood everywhere.

"I went into the kitchen and got some socks from the wicker basket to wear as gloves, so there were no fingerprints.

"Then I went upstairs to get a blanket and found two small children sleeping in the bedroom. They couldn't have been more than five and seven years old.

"I couldn't believe what I was seeing. The apartment belong to Carol Skinner, we called her Blonde Carol. She'd gone out and the Krays were the childminders.

"I took a deep breath, tiptoed in and got the blanket. Then I snuck out and wrapped Jack in the blanket.

"We tidied up and I was walking upstairs with a bucket of blood to pour it down the toilet when Blonde Carol came back with her boyfriend.

"I told her there had been a bit of a kerfuffle but everything was being taken care of. I told her to go into the bedroom and wait with her children until we were gone."

It wasn't the first time the Krays were trusted to babysit

Ex-EastEnders star Jamie Foreman remembers them looking after him at their snooker hall while his father Freddie, an enforcer for the twins, did their dirty work.

And Freddie Foreman soon found himself dragged into disposing of the body - and the fall out that followed.

The Lambrianou brothers reluctantly agreed to help the Krays' driver Ronnie Bender take the body south of the river and dump it on a railway line so a train would obliterate it.

But McVitie's body was too big to fit into the boot of his car. So Tony would drive McVitie's car with the bleeding corpse on the back seat.

Lambrianou would follow in his car with Bender.

Lambrianou says: "I was hoping the nightmare wouldn't get any worse, but it did. We were sat at a red light when a police car with two officers in pulled up behind Tony.

"I thought they were going to pull him over.
"There was no way I was going to let Tony take the rap for a murder he didn't commit.
"I had a gun in his pocket, so there I was, ready to kill two policemen and orphan their kids to save him."
Luckily the police car turned off at the next junction and Tony was allowed to drive on until the car ran out of petrol outside a church in Rotherhithe, deep in Foreman's territory.

Foreman later collected the body and dumped it in the sea off Newhaven in East Sussex.
The remains were never found, but that wasn't enough to save the gang.
Everyone connected to the murder was arrested by Met detective "Nipper" Reid and stood trial at the Old Bailey as the Krays' violent empire came crumbling down.

Chris Lambrianou

Kray twins filmmakers are blasted by niece of Reggie's tragic first wife who caught the crime boss's eye as a teenager and died of an overdose

The family of Reggie Kray's first wife has criticised the new biopic about the notorious East End gangster twins starring Tom Hardy.

The movie, Legend, sees Hardy play both Reggie and Ronnie Kray, with Emily Browning as Reggie's young wife Frances Shea.

Now, her niece, also named Frances Shea, says the portrayal of her late aunt in the film upset her and her daughter to the point where they were forced to walk out of the screening.

Ms Shea, 52, and her daughter, Bonny Frances, 26, from London, also criticise the production team behind Legend for not contacting the Shea family while doing their research for the upcoming blockbuster film.

Frances Shea, known to family as Franie, met Reggie at the age of 16 and married him five years later, in a ceremony that filled the tabloid pages.

However, their 1965 wedding was the beginning of the end to their relationship, and Franie left Reggie within a matter of weeks, officially ending the marriage eight months later.

According to her family, Franie suffered from mental health issues, took her own life by overdosing medication in 1967, just 23 years old. Although it is widely accepted that she committed suicide, according to one account, Franie was murdered by Ronnie Kray, for reasons that are unclear.

News to them: The Shea family say they were unaware of what a large role Franie, pictured on her wedding day with Reggie, left, and Ronnie, right, would play in the film

Critical: Her niece, also named Frances, say the Legend team did not contact them while doing their research for the Tom Hardy blockbuster and have not told Franie' story with respect for the Shea family

Tragic: Frances Shea, pictured with Ronnie (left) and Reggie Kray (right) on her wedding day in April 1965, suffered mental health issues and took her own life just two years after the wedding

Reggie Kray with his girlfriend Frances (Frankie) Shea

40 years on the run

He was the man who brought down the Krays, but the moment Bobby Teale decided to betray the vicious twins he knew he was signing his own death warrant.

The former henchman had seen enough of the sadistic violence meted out by the East End thugs during their reign of terror and wanted to bring it to an end – even though he was fully aware of the consequences of double-crossing the notorious duo.

And after his evidence helped put Ronnie and Reggie behind bars for the rest of their days, Bobby had no choice but to flee, knowing if he stuck around at best he would get a bullet in the head and, at worst, be mercilessly tortured before being murdered.

So he went on the run for 40 years.

Now, in an exclusive interview, the 70-year-old reveals how he decided to turn supergrass after Ronnie started making sickening sexual advances towards his 11-year-old brother Paul. He even thought about killing the crime lo ord himself if he touched the youngster, meaning instant death at the hands of Kray heavies in the room.

The incident happened in his brother David's flat in Clapton, East London, in 1966.

Ronnie was hiding out there after murdering rival George Cornell.

Bobby recalls: "Ronnie announced he wanted Paul to sit on his lap. I went to the kitchen and got my gun from where I'd left it on top of the fridge.

"If Ronnie made a move on Paul, that would be his last. I was intending to unload the gun on him.

"I hid it under my coat and, taking a deep breath, I stood in the doorway of the living room. I intended to empty the six bullets into him.

"I also knew that if I did let Ronnie have what was coming, I would not get out alive

Ronnie then told his entourage he was going for a "lie down" and tried to steer young Paul towards the bedroom.

Bobby blocked his path, and after a terrifying stand-off in the doorway, Kray backed down.

But he knew the gangster, who had raped and abused a string of young men, never stopped until he got what he wanted.

He said: "As soon as he went for my brother I knew I couldn't walk away.

"My stomach was churning but I had made up my mind what I was about to do, even though I could hardly believe it myself."I phoned Scotland Yard from a call box near my mum's flat."

Reunited: Bobby, centre, with brothers David and Alfie

The 30 second call set in motion a chain of events that would lead to the arrest of Ronnie, Reggie and members of their gang.

Bobby, David and his other brother Alfie, also friends of the Krays, would testify against them at Court One of the Old Bailey.

When the twins were convicted of two murders in 1969 and sentenced to a minimum 30 years in jail, it was largely the Teales' evidence which put them there.

The trial also meant a life sentence of another sort for married Bobby, then a handsome 23-year-old from North London.

For the next four decades he vanished, leaving his wife behind and escaping to Canada and later the US where he started a new life and family.

He missed his parents' funerals before coming back from the dead two years ago when he responded to a Facebook appeal that Alfie, now 72, and David, 69, launched in a bid to make contact.

Bobby had only recently told his new family in America about his past.

One Christmas, daughter Paula gave him a coffee table book called Defining Moments in History in which he spotted a picture of Reggie's funeral.

Bobby said: "I felt a sudden torrent of emotion. Trying to hide it, I stood up and got the attention of the family, saying casually, 'See the man in this coffin? He was once my best friend'.

" " "

David turned Ronnie away at the club door one night only to be told by his brother: "Do you know who that is? You can't do that to Ronnie Kray." " " "

"The kids were shocked. 'Who is it?' they asked. 'His name was Reggie Kray,' I said softly, 'and he was one of the most notorious criminals of his time.

"He had a twin brother called Ronnie. I helped bring them down'."

One of his children asked: "Dad, if you were his friend, does that mean you were a criminal too?"

Bobby, who lives in Utah, decided it was time to write a book about his amazing experiences so his children and grandkids would know the truth.

His research dredged up painful memories he had suppressed for years. In the 60s, when the Krays lorded it over London's criminal underworld, Bobby's mother ran a club in Islington, North London.

That was how his family first became linked to the twin

Bobby, now 70, says: "I didn't know how to reply. There was a long silence. Eventually my daughter said softly, 'Dad, did you ever kill anyone?' 'The opposite,' I said.

"'I tried to save people, and I suffered for it'."

Bobby had never mentioned his secret life to his family but now he felt it was time to tell his story and set the record straight about the Kray twins.

He recalls: "I saw things that terrified and disgusted me, things that I would never want to know about. I had to make a stand. I did something that put my own life in danger.

"I had to run away from my old life and let my family think I was dead. Anger and grief welled up and I slammed the book shut."

Ronnie, who ran the Two Rs club in Bethnal Green with Reggie, said he wanted to do business with the Teales. The brothers insist they were never on the payroll of The Firm but they were soon required to entertain the Krays and run errands for them.

In their time with the twins, all three witnessed savage beatings and the results of Ronnie's wild mood swings. Bobby's book is filled with tales of the Krays' reign of terror. It punctures the myth that has for decades painted them as honourable East End heroes.

For three years from 1966, while a trusted figure at the heart of the brothers' empire, Bobby betrayed the gangsters' code by feeding vital information to Scotland Yard under the codename Phillips.

Details of the Krays' activities allowed police to build a detailed picture of how extensive their grip on the British underworld was.

But all the time the twins were getting word from bent police officers that Phillips was providing information. Bobby believes he was on the point of being exposed a number of times.

Describing one, he says: "We were all in a very small crowded room with Ronnie and Reggie and someone came in and said, 'Phillips has been on the phone again'.

"It was a set up by Ronnie. He had orchestrated it so he could watch everyone's reaction.

"He started glaring at each member of The Firm and then he came to me but I put on a dozy look like I was listening to the person next to me.

"When Ronnie got to my face there was no reaction and I knew if there was I would be dead.

"I knew each move I made was possibly my last. There was nothing else I could do. I was never going to live through this but I will do what I can to help my family."
And if there was any doubt about what would happen to Bobby if the twins found he was the grass, it ended with the fate of a low-life criminal known as Frosty.
Crooked police officers were leaking information about Phillips back to the Krays, so Bobby asked his police handler to release some false intelligence to help protect him.
He had told them about Frosty, who had previously boasted about raping and killing a young girl, and murdering another man with an axe.
Bobby says: "At last I could see the Yard at work. Soon after they let a leak out saying Frosty was Phillips.
"When Ronnie heard via the Yard informer the crook was the grass, he killed him.

"Ronnie Kray tortured him to death, poor b******, trying to get him to tell them what he had told the police.
"And he'd told them nothing. His body was never found."
But Bobby did live to give evidence against the Krays who fixed him with stares in court as they finally realised who had betrayed them.
He says: "I don't believe they learned who Phillips was until the last minute."
Sitting in a London pub 43 years later, Bobby says:
"There is a quote from somewhere I've always remembered, 'All that is necessary for evil to triumph is that good men do nothing'.
"I had to do something and I did it, even at the terrible cost of losing my family for 40 years. I'm not ashamed of that. I'm proud of it."

Ronnie Kray was always suited and booted for my visits to see him in Broadmoor. All that was missing was the tiny pistol called a "mutt gun" he used to tuck in his sock.

The gun, like his gold watches, Armani ties and the bayonet he used on victims, are all going up for auction tomorrow.

They came into my possession shortly after I met Ron in 1988, and married him a year later. And despite our divorce they've remained with me after he died in 1995, aged 61, while serving a life sentence in the psychiatric hospital.

How did I come by all these things? I'll always remember one associate, Charlie Clarke – who was later killed – dropping off a huge tea chest. It was full of Ron's stuff from before he went inside in 1968. I used to have other gangsters come to my door with a box or case and say: "The Colonel said you had to have this."

I guess it was Ron's way of moving in with me, though he never expected to leave Broadmoor.

And mark my words, despite his treatment there the dark side never left him. "Never apologise, Kate," he'd tell me. "Not when you wanted to do it."

I remember the chill I felt when he told me he liked the look in George Cornell's eyes as he shot him dead in the Blind Beggar pub in the East End.

There were also times I saw Ron in a rage, when the drugs controlling his schizophrenia needed topping up. I first met him because his brother Reggie asked me to take Ron a letter in Broadmoor. Ron charmed me on that first visit and proposed on the second. We married there and he looked a million dollars. But Reggie was the most important thing in Ron's life and some of the personal messages I delivered from one to the other are going up for sale too, along with more than 100 other items.

I know many will say I'm cashing in on a violent criminal – and he could be chilling –but I don't see it that way. Recently I gave a talk after the Krays were chosen along with the likes of William Hogarth and Michael Faraday as among 32 Londoners who shaped the capital.

Smart: Kray's Black Dinner Jacket

ou'd think all these suits are from when the twins were in their gangland heyday. Ron did probably have nights out with Diana Dors and Barbara Windsor in the dinner jacket with velvet lapels, above, but he wore the green Lester Bowden sports jacket, inset, in Broadmoor. Because it's a hospital not a prison, inmates wear their own clothes. And Ron took advantage of this privilege.

He had his tailors go in to measure him up for Italian-cut suits. I'd get them dry-cleaned but he got inmates to iron his shirts and polish his shoes. He refused to see people if they came in jeans or their shoes weren't shiny.

I gave him a Giorgio Armani tie. He sent me to Russell & Bromley to get crocodile shoes. He'd say: "Don't worry if the size isn't quite right, I've hardly got far to walk."

Ron was known to use bayonets on his victims... We don't know and don't want to know if this one was used. The "mutt gun" was a small pistol he kept in his right sock.

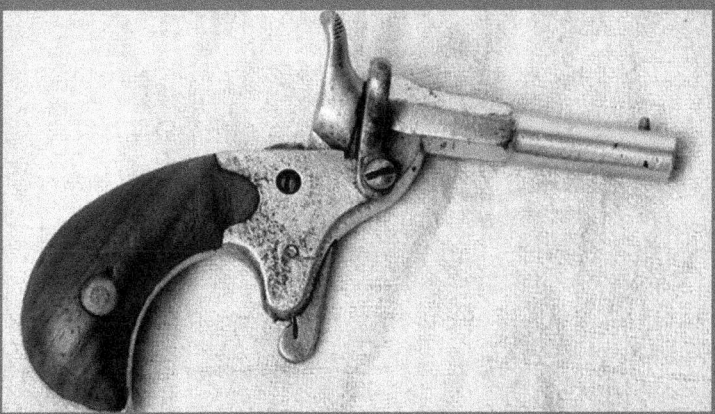

Ron told me he had this by his bed.
You can see it's a clock but what Ron
loved was the canary.
He'd had a real canary in his cell in
Parkhurst and doted on it. He had
lots of things other prisoners would
never be allowed.

Next to my picture on Ron's bedside table were these in this leather frame. It has plastic over it because he wasn't allowed glass in his cell. Until her death in 1982, he spoke to his mum Violet after every episode of Coronation Street.

THREAT TO SOCIETY OR SPENT FORCE OF EVIL..

Is it time to free Reggie Kray?

Statement from Reg kray

I MADE many mistakes over the years and one of these was springing Frank "The Mad Axeman" Mitchell from Dartmoor, where he was serving a life sentence for holding an old couple captive while he sat over them holding an axe balanced on his knee.

Ron and I had met Frank years before when we did time together in Wandsworth.

He was a big, powerful man whom no one could control, mainly because he had the mind of a child and if he didn't get his own way he'd kick off. With someone of his size that caused many problems for the authorities, so much so that they shoved him into Broadmoor and Rampton on a few occasions. But he was a likeable fella in a childish sort of way.

After we'd done our time in Wandsworth, which had only been six months for GBH, Frank kept in touch with Ronnie. Letter after letter arrived at Vallance Road and because Ronnie was no letter writer, most of the time it was Mum who answered them.

They were all mostly in the same vein with Frank complaining that the Home Office would not give him a release date, which all prisoners want because it gives them something to work towards. Eventually Ronnie got it in to his head that it would be doing Frank a favour if we got him out of Dartmoor.

If you were a mental patient and got out of the hospital and stayed at large for some time without getting into trouble the authorities that had put you there had to reconsider your position. I am sure this was in the back of Ronnie's mind. Why I let myself get talked into it I don't know but when Ronnie got a bee in his bonnet he could be very persuasive.

I came round in the end, thinking if nothing else it would stick two fingers up to the law, which we'd been doing since we were kids. Getting out of Dartmoor was not quite accurate because most of Frank's days were spent outside the walls anyway. The screws found him easier to control if he was left to his own devices and that meant allowing him to wander around on the moor and even pop into a local pub with a screw keeping an eye on him.

o lifting him would be no problem. To set the plan in action I got old-time boxer Ted "Kid" Lewis to offer to go in to the prison and give a talk while showing boxing films. The governor loved the idea and of course I stuck a hat on and a pair of heavy glasses and accompanied Ted in disguise.

This gave me a chance to have a word with Frank and fill him in on what we planned. A week later I sent Albert Donoghue, "Mad" Tommy Smith and Billy Exley to pick Frank up at a prearranged location. It was as simple as that and even before he was reported missing he was safely in a flat in Canning Town.

Apart from Ron and I being busy we'd heard that Frank was making a nuisance of himself so we didn't go round to see him. We'd done what we'd set out to do and as far as we were concerned that was that. We heard that he wanted to go up West to find himself a girl and we couldn't let that happen because without a shadow of a doubt, being as conspicuous as he was, he'd have been picked up in five minutes.

"" I've no regrets about killing Jack The Hat because he was the most vexatious person I'd come across""

So we arranged for one of our girls from the Winston club to go round to the flat and keep him company. That kept him quiet for a while but then he started complaining he wasn't being shown respect because we weren't spending time with him and he was bored in the flat. More and more he was threatening to come to Vallance Road to find us.

We had three choices. Hand him to the police, in which case he would point the finger at us. Let him leave, whereupon he'd be lifted and again put us in the frame or, the third option, which really was the only solution to our problem before it all went pearshaped, we'd have him killed.
With the idea in place we didn't hang about. I got in touch with Alfie Gerrard and another couple of the chaps who would sort out Frank, who was told he was going to be taken into the country where he would meet up with Ronnie.

Not that this was the only thing that put me in my present predicament but it was certainly the catalyst. I hear talk that I was egged on to do what I did by Ronnie, supposedly saying: 'I've done one, now it's your turn.' This was not the case at all. What happened was a very spur-of-the-moment thing and was really brought about by Jack himself.
There was a time when Jack was not a bad bloke but as time went on he began to drink heavily and was sniffing the white powder. While he was sober he was OK but when not, he turned into big trouble. We had paid him £1,500 to carry out a job but he never saw it through and kept the money. Then he started to cause trouble wherever he went and we were getting complaints from club owners who were under our protection. Ronnie and I gave him warnings but he never took any notice, so something had to be done.

Ronnie and Reggie Kray had a secret incestuous relationship with each other

vicious gangster twins Ronnie and Reggie Kray had an incestuous sexual relationship with each other as they were growing up.

The pair, who ran a cruel and violent criminal empire in London's East End in the 1960s, were terrified of their secret coming out.

They were worried that rivals would see their sexuality – Ronnie was a homosexual and Reggie was bisexual - as a sign of weakness so only had sex with each other in order to keep the secret.

"Homosexuality was nothing to be proud of in the East End.

"But as they became more notorious, Ronnie became quite shameless about it.

"According to Ron in the early days they had sex with each other because they were terrified about people finding out."

It has long been known that Ronnie was a homosexual and Reggie was bisexual but the news they had a sexual relationship with each other gives a telling insight into their close connection.

Ron wore wideframed glasses like these. He had a tortoiseshell pair like mine. He knew quality but he'd been inside so long he didn't know modern fashions

Reg kray ((top))
reg in 1982 ((left))
reg and ron at the wedding
1965

Legendary Daily Mirror feature writer Paul Callan on his chilling prison interviews with violent twins Ronnie and Reggie Kray, how they confessed to murder and confirms Tom Hardy has captured their menace perfectly in his new film

It was when Ronnie Kray lowered his voice to a hard, even-toned whisper that you detected the menace. His eyes suddenly grew black and he leaned forward across the small, plastic-topped table, his face just inches from your own.

"George Cornell?" he said, as if jeering at the very name. "He was a drunkard and a bully and I done him. Me – not my brother."

Cornell, a violent gangster who openly mocked the Kray twins, met his end while sitting at the bar of the London East End pub The Blind Beggar, on March 9, 1966.

Word had reached the Krays that the thuggish Cornell had called Ronnie "a big fat poof" – an insult that guaranteed his death sentence. Thus Ronnie never hesitated that evening at exactly 8.30pm. Despite a taunting cry of "Look what the dog has dragged in" from Cornell, Ronnie calmly took a 9mm Luger from his pocket and shot him once in the forehead.

There was an icy pause, then a light triumphant smile as Ronnie remembered the scene. Then he added with visible relish: "I done the earth a favour..."

Strong memories of my interview with Ronnie returned forcibly to me this week when I watched a screening of Legend, a new film about the Krays in which the brilliant Tom Hardy plays both brothers.

I interviewed the twins – Ronnie in Broadmoor in 1983 and Reggie three years later in Parkhurst Prison – at a time when they were near to having served 20 years of their sentences.

For anyone, like me, who spent even a short time with these infamous brothers who had held London in a grip with their murderous protection rackets, it was chillingly clear that Tom Hardy has captured their stomach-churning air of murderous intent.

The hard stares, the icy tones of their voices, and the manner in which they assessed you – everything was there. It was like being back in their presence thirty-odd years ago.

Ronnie, the older by 45 minutes was 48 when I met him in Broadmoor, the grim, Victorian high security psychiatric hospital in Berkshire. I joined others on visiting day and, although I had not sought permission from the Home Office, I was able to take notes without being noticed.

The very fact that I was writing down Ronnie's observations appeared to please him. It gave him a sense of importance and when another "patient" (as prisoners are called at Broadmoor) approached us, Ronnie waved him away,

"I'm being interviewed by the Daily Mirror," he said. "Don't bother us just now."

Judging by his appearance incarceration seemed to agree with him. His light blue pleated shirt fitted him easily and his blue check 60-ish style trousers were snug around the hips.

He had a clean, almost scrubbed look about him and the raven black hair carried only wisps of grey. A heavy gold Rolex watch hung from his left wrist and he half smoked Benson and Hedges cigarettes, grinding their last seconds into an old tobacco tin.

His fingers were fussily-manicured – ironically, not the hands of a killer, but of an artist. He liked to paint, he said, and even offered to send me one of his landscapes.

His long, pointed face, dominated by a squarish nose, was close and the occasionally wary eyes drilled hard into you.

He spoke of his early days "inside" when depression often enveloped him. "But now I take it all easy. All easy like," he said.

"I keep fit with a lot of exercise – particularly walking." Then he allowed himself a little joke. "But not right out of the gate." There was the shadow of a smile.

Then came a surprising admission. "I love opera? Do you? Maria Callas, Gigli. Lovely stuff. My favourite is Madam Buttterfly. And I like that big bloke, Pavarotti. Can you send me a tape of him singing? I'd like that."

He still felt close to his brother and harboured deep anger that Reggie was still a Category A prisoner. His eyes darkened.

"I understand to a point why I've got to do a long time in prison," he said. "But not my brother. Not Reggie.

"He never done no murders. I done them. Reg is innocent." You could almost smell the seething resentment.

He was, by now, clearly furious. "We never harmed no one on the outside. No 'civilians'. We kept to our own people.

"We got 30 years. But they let people who do sex crimes and things to little children out after a few years. Is that fair?"

He calmed down and sipped a (non-alcoholic) lager. Suddenly, he asked: "Do you know Judy Garland? She came to see me. And Diana Dors, she's been here and that boxer John Conteh. Lovely fella...."

In their hey-day the twins entertained many celebrities and when I mentioned that Liza Minnelli was performing in London, his faced brightened.

"Do you think she'd come and see me? I'd love that," he said. Our conversation finally led to sex and he prodded my notebook with his forefinger. "I want you to write this down – and I want you to say that I am proud to have Jewish blood and that I am also proud to be homosexual. Have you got that?"

Ronnie kept glancing nervously at his Rolex, as if time was closing in on him. Then a shrill bell announced the end of visiting time and he gave me a parting iron hand grip.

"Promise you'll come back again," he said, almost child-like, and added quietly: "If you see my brother Reggie, tell him I'm happy. Yeah happy."

And he went led tenderly away.

I was able to pass on that message three years later when, after much intricate arranging, I interviewed Reggie in Parkhurst Prison.

Here was a man who exuded strength and hideous violence. There was a presence about him – one that was readily recognised by other prisoners.

He personified power and all around other convicts stood as he passed by. The visiting wives, some with sad, drained faces, smiled at him and a couple even touched his hand.

He was bigger, more muscular than Ronnie and he sported a grey sweat-shirt with the word "Lonsdale" across his boxer's chest. In their youth, the twins were promising in the ring – and could easily have been contenders.

We chatted about the old days and I ventured the view that he and his brother had terrified a lot of people. Did he regret it?

He gave a thin smile. "Yeah, I do regret some of them things. And I do know I did frighten quite a lot people." Reggie wanted these questions to go away and his eyes grew hard behind the blue-tinted glasses. "I don't allow myself to live in the past," he said.

I persisted. "But how many people did you kill?" Now those dark eyes registered danger and I was glad a couple of prison officers were nearby.

"Look," he said in a threatening whisper, "that's a libellous question. I'm in here for one murder."

Then he openly admitted for the first time ever that he had murdered Jack "The Hat" McVitie, another evil hoodlum who fell foul of the twins.

"Yeah, I killed McVitie. He had boasted he was going to kill me with a shot gun. So it was really self-defence." But was he pointing a gun at you at the time? "No," said Reggie. "But I heard he was going to kill me – so I killed him. I stabbed him with a knife.

"He deserved it. Once, he stabbed someone in a club and came upstairs and wiped the knife on some women's dresses."

"""There followed a lengthy pause. Then he said, with a noisy laugh: "Well, he wasn't such a nice guy, was he?"""

He had, like Ronnie, a lingering affection for the good old days when it was considered smart to be seen with the Krays. Socialites, MPs and members of the House of Lords and many a star, liked the dangerous charisma that rubbed off on them. It was hoodlum chic. They were even photographed by celebrity photographer David Bailey.

"Yeah, he was a nice geezer," said Reggie. "Good days." The last time I saw the twins was when they were let out for the funeral of their formidable mother Violet, to whom they were particularly close.

Even they looked surprised at the numbers who turned up to see them arrive for a funeral service at Chingford Old Church in Essex.

But the authorities were determined the twins were not seen in any heroic light. They were accompanied by extra tall prison officers who towered over them, making these one time giants of villainy look small. Death finally caught up with them – Ronnie in 1995 and Reggie five years later. Sentencing them in 1969 at the Old Bailey, Mr Justice Melford Stevenson said, with scornful understatement: "In my view, society has earned a rest from your activities."

But as the new film proves, their legend, steeped in evil, lives on.

My Date with the Reg Kray

HMP Parkhurst

Which is how, as a young journalist in London in the 1990s, I found myself en route to Parkhurst to interview Reggie Kray.

Parkhurst was a maximum security institution, and journalists were not allowed to wander in and out chatting to inmates. Understandable, really.

Especially since the detainee in question had once controlled the London underworld, when he and his brother Ronnie were synonymous with a perverted form of celebrity known as gangster chic.

An arrangement was made for me to visit the Isle of Wight prison with a former girlfriend of Kray's – a preserved dolly bird, who met me at the train station. My escort spent the journey fantasising about setting up home with him after he was freed. But he had no release date from his life sentence for murder, even after almost three decades. That's why he was interested in talking to the press: he was lobbying to get out.

At Parkhurst – a grim 19th century building which could never be mistaken for anything but a place of detention – we were searched, then led to a room full of visitors. A door in the far wall opened, and a group of prisoners and warders appeared.

Among the first to arrive was a wiry little jockey of a man; instantly familiar, but considerably older looking than the iconic 1960s portrait of him with his twin.

Reggie Kray bolted straight towards me, quivering with purposeful energy. He may have been short, but he was strong. I was grabbed by the upper arms, lifted off the ground and a thumping great smacker planted on my lips. Time slowed right down. I dangled there, being kissed by him, for what seemed rather a long time. I could taste the nicotine on his breath. Thoughts floated through my mind. First came: 'A notorious gangland killer has his mouth glued to mine.' Followed by: 'How can I make this stop?'

Still, I learned one useful lesson – if you want an interviewer rendered incapable of tricky questions, just snog him or her right off. Turns the brain to mush.

Which probably explains why I don't remember much about our conversation, apart from having some Cockney rhyming slang explained to me. He also mentioned his twin Ronnie, incarcerated in Broadmoor, for the criminally insane – but not in terms of brotherly love. With the benefit of hindsight, not to mention several decades lodging at Her Majesty's pleasure, he regarded Ronnie as a bad influence. My clearest memory is of being glowered at by a handsome young bodybuilder inmate, with collar-length silky blonde hair. He watched us moodily throughout. Later, I learned he was Kray's cellmate, and they were particularly close.

Reggie Kray sent me several letters afterwards, inviting me back to Parkhurst. You never saw such spidery handwriting, with a very free attitude to the use of capitals and to running words along straight lines. I never replied. These missives didn't come to my office, you see – he sent them to my home address.

A few weeks later, I was assigned to interview a handwriting analyst, and brought along one of the letters without identifying its author. The moment he touched the page, the expert dropped it as though his finger tips were scorched. 'Have nothing to do with this dangerous person,' he urged. I didn't need telling twice.

But some people aren't easy to shake off. Soon after, my Parkhurst travelling companion arrived at my flat – did everyone in the East End have my address? She had a message from Reggie: he wanted her to bring me back to see him. Tentatively, expecting resistance, I said I wasn't particularly keen. Relief flooded her face. She agreed it would be best if I stayed away, and volunteered to sort it out with Reggie.

'What will you tell him?' I asked. 'Don't worry, dahlin', I'll fink of something.' Whatever she came up with proved effective. I never heard from Reggie Kray again.

I did hear, however, that he was released from prison a few years later in the year 2000, on compassionate grounds he had cancer, and it was at an advanced stage. Just over a month after being freed, he died.

The other day I came across one of his letters, and realised I had his autograph at the bottom of the page, squiggly but legible. But that wasn't all. It came complete with three towering big Xs. Even on the page, they carried a wallop.
Love from Reggie Kray, kiss, kiss, kiss.

Martina Devlin is a bestselling author and award-winning journalist.

Tribute: Ronnie Kray as he attends the funeral of his mother Violet at Chingford Mount Cemetery at Chingford, Essex

Reggie Kray as he attends the funeral of his mother Violet at Chingford Mount Cemetery at Chingford, Essex

If there was one British actor who could simultaneously bring to life the UK's most famous gangster twins, it was always going to be Tom Hardy.

And the Hollywood star certainly looked the parts in the first film still from The Krays biopic, Legend. Wearing the glasses and three-piece suit of Ronnie on one side, while smoking a cigarette as Reggie on the other, even in this single shot one can see how Tom has defined each character.

The film also stars Emily Browning, David Thewlis and Christopher Eccleston but the supporting cast have yet to be seen on the east London set, which continued filming on Thursday.

Wearing prosthetics and vintage suits, Tom's stand-in was dressed as Reggie to help the crew set up shots for the main talent at Turner's Old Star pub.

The artist Joseph Mallard William Turner was rumoured to be the owner of the watering hole, and it is though that he often visited the place of debauchery under the pseudonym 'Admiral Puggy Booth'.

No doubt, the pub is a resonant choice for the film which chronicles the life of two of the most notorious gangsters in British history who grew up and operated primarily from the East End.

Ronnie and Reggie were born on 25 October 1933 in Hoxton, and first attended Wood Close School in Brick Lane before going onto Daniel Street School. In 1938, the Kray family moved from Hoxton to Bethnal Green, at 178 Vallance Road, which is certainly not far from Turner's Old Star.

At Cannes this year there was a lot of interest in the film, with the response from buyers that it 'was one of the best scripts' they'd come across.

Confirming the news in April, Tom said: 'I'm on that right now. I've got to work out how to play both twins, which will be fun. It's another experiment and I'm really looking forward to it.

'I'm not going to put too much pressure on myself, I just want to have some fun. The more of a challenge I give myself, the easier it is to take on more projects which are complicated in the future.'

The Hollywood hunk previously told MailOnline that he was keen to take on the roles as he said: 'All the plans are on the table.

'There's a lot of crossing the t's and dotting the i's, and there's a lot of shift and geography to work out.'

From a screenplay penned by LA Confidential writer, Brian Helgeland, the story will focus on the Kray twins' wheelings and illegal dealings during the fifties and sixties, with Hardy playing both brothers.

'It would be difficult,' Tom said about the mechanics of playing two characters sharing a lot of the same screen time. 'It's quite technical and I'm a bit of an anorak.'

He added: 'There's a physical transfer; we'd have to shoot one bit, go away come back and shoot it all again with another part. I've never dreamt of playing two people on the screen!'

Hardy is expected to portray the struggle of the elder brother Reggie to keep in check the unstable actions of his younger twin, rumoured to have been a paranoid schizophrenic.

As heads of the notorious criminal gang The Firm, the Krays were behind numerous armed robberies, murders, arson attacks and protection rackets up until their arrest on 9th May 1968.

Their story was previously told on film in the 1990s, with real life brothers Martin and Gary Kemp playing the title roles.

The Oscar-winning screenwriter's script doesn't just concern the criminals that the brothers dealt with, but also the likes of Frank Sinatra, Judy Garland and other celebrities, who frequented their former Knightsbridge nightclub Esmeralda's Barn, which is now the site of the Berkeley Hotel.

It is also said to look at Ronnie's alleged sexual relationship with two British politicians; Lord Boothby, a UK Conservative Party politician, and, Labour MP Tom Driberg.

Of course, playing a violent former boxer-turned-criminal won't be too tough a feat for Hardy, who proved his worth as the title character in Nicolas Winding Refn's biopic Bronson.

And he continued down the gangster path with his role in BBC period crime drama Peaky Blinders, opposite his Inception co-star Cillian Murphy.

Disguise: Tom was barely unrecognisable as he filmed scenes as the Kray twins

Start of the 60's

At the start of the 60's all the brothers were together again, Ron was getting back to his old self, the Firm had truly established itself, business was good and they were making inroads into the West End gambling and club scene.

Their first toehold in this area was an upmarket gaming club called Esmeraldas. It was fronted by Lord Effingham, the sixth Earl of Effingham. He was paid by the Krays to welcome the customers as they entered the club.

they also invested a lot of their own money in a seaside development in a place called Enugu in Nigeria. It was set up by their business manager Leslie Payne and Ernest Shinwell, son of Manny Shinwell, a labour MP. The Initial introduction into the project took place between Ronnie, a man called Leslie Holt

and Lord Boothby, a Peer of The Realm. In the end the project collapsed and the money disappeared.

Later, Leslie Holt was to die under very strange circumstances and another disappeared never to be seen again.

Ronnie Kray met Lord Boothby through one of the many gay parties that they both attended. He realised he was gay at a very early age when he fell in love with a boy across the road from where he lived. He didn't hide his sexuality but it wasn't until the sexual freedom of the sixties that it became widely known.

The Krays were mixing with some very influential people and, it was thought, by some, that they were getting too powerful. They were being watched constantly by the Authorities.

One of the reasons for their eventual downfall was their love of publicity. Ronnie in particular loved being photographed with celebrities and sports stars, He wanted to display himself as the stereotypical American Gangster as portrayed by James Cagney and George Raft in the American films of the 50's and 60's. The difference between The Krays and their real life, American counterparts, the Mafia, is that they kept a low profile and let others do their dirty work.

In 1965 the Twins were arrested for demanding money with menaces from a man called Hew McGowan, the owner of a club called the Hideaway. They were remanded in custody to Brixton prison.

Their influence was so wide reaching that questions were asked in the House of Lords as to how long they were going to keep the Twins locked up. These questions, asked by Lord Boothby, caused a sensation. When they went to court they were cleared of all charges.

In less than a month they owned the Hideaway club and changed the name to El Morocco.

Also in April, 1965, Reggie married the love of his life, Francis Shea, the sister of his good friend Frank. She was twenty one years old. It was a marriage which would end in disaster. 8 months later they were living apart much to Reggie's disappointment.

Ronnie and Reggie were now forging links with the Mafia. They went to America for a week and met their top men. Although they made some very useful connections on their trip, they didn't do as much business as they thought they would. They did however, provide protection, on behalf of the Mafia, for many American celebrities visiting or performing in England. And protected their gambling interests in the West End as well as entertaining them when they came to London..

The Krays shared control of London with the Richardson gang from South London. The main body of the Richardson gang consisted of, brothers, Charlie and Eddie, 'Mad' Frankie Fraser and George Cornell. They were already entrenched in the West End, supplying most of the clubs with one armed bandits, and the Krays wanted in

In March 1966 a gun battle took place in a club called Mr Smiths in Rushey Green. It has been said that The Richardson gang went there with the intentions of wiping out the Krays. There was only one member of the Kray gang present. He was shot dead. Frankie Fraser was shot in the hip and Eddie was shot in the backside. They were taken to hospital and on their release they were charged with affray and sentenced to 5 years in prison. Frankie Fraser was originally charged with the murder of Dickie Hart but was found not guilty.

Frankie Fraser 1966

The curtains were kept drawn now where the krays had frank mitchell a escaped prisoner . Ronnie remind a prisoner locking himself away from the police he was armed and very dangerious going mad from solitude he was certain men at large seeking revenage for cornell . he had to kill them first. they were all on his list. as he lay on his bed locked in his bedroom he planned exactly how to kill each one of them.life was a waking nightmare for him then. his violent life had turned against him

Ronnie Kray pictured here had

Paranoid
Schizophrenia

Paranoid schizophrenia, also called **schizophrenia, paranoid type** is a sub-type of schizophrenia as defined in the Diagnostic and Statistical Manual of Mental Disorders, DSM-IV code 295.30. It is the most common type of schizophrenia. Schizophrenia is defined as "a chronic mental disorder in which a person loses touch with reality (psychosis)." Schizophrenia is divided into subtypes based on the "predominant symptomatology at the time of evaluation." The clinical picture is dominated by relatively stable and often persecutory delusions that are usually accompanied by hallucinations, particularly of the auditory variety (hearing voices), and perceptual disturbances. These symptoms can have a huge effect on functioning and can negatively affect quality of life. Paranoid schizophrenia is a lifelong disease, but with proper treatment, a person with the illness can attain a higher quality of life.

A work of outsider art made by a person with paranoid schizophrenia.

Example of delusional obsession with numbers in paranoid schizophrenic.

Although paranoid schizophrenia is defined by those two symptoms, it is also defined by a lack of certain symptoms (negative symptoms). The following symptoms are not prominent: "disorganized speech, disorganized or catatonic behavior, or flat or inappropriate affect." Those symptoms are present in another form of schizophrenia, disorganized-type schizophrenia.

The criteria for diagnosing paranoid schizophrenia must be present from at least one to six months. This helps to differentiate schizophrenia from other illnesses, such as bipolar disorder.

Paranoid schizophrenia is defined in the Diagnostic and Statistical Manual of Mental Disorders, 4th Edition, but it was dropped from the 5th Edition. The American Psychiatric Association chose to eliminate schizophrenia subtypes because they had "limited diagnostic stability, low reliability, and poor validity." The symptoms and lack of symptoms that were being used to categorize the different subtypes of schizophrenia were not concrete enough to be able to be diagnosed.

The APA also believed that the subtypes of schizophrenia should be removed because "they did not appear to help with providing better targeted treatment, or predicting treatment response. Targeted treatment and treatment response vary from patient to patient, depending on his or her symptoms. It is more beneficial, therefore, to look at the severity of the symptoms when considering treatment options.

Paranoid schizophrenia manifests itself in an array of symptoms. Common symptoms for paranoid schizophrenia include auditory hallucinations (hearing voices) and paranoid delusions (believing everyone is out to cause the sufferer harm. However, two of the symptoms separate this form of schizophrenia from other forms.

One criterion for separating paranoid schizophrenia from other types is delusion. A delusion is a belief that is held strong even when the evidence shows otherwise. Some common delusions associated with paranoid schizophrenia include, "believing that the government is monitoring every move you make, or that a co-worker is poisoning your lunch." In all but rare cases, these beliefs are irrational, and can cause the person holding them to behave abnormally. Another frequent type of delusion is a delusion of grandeur, or the "fixed, false belief that one possesses superior qualities such as genius, fame, omnipotence, or wealth." Common ones include, "the belief that you can fly, that you're famous, or that you have a relationship with a famous person."

Another criterion present in patients with paranoid schizophrenia is auditory hallucinations, in which the person hears voices or sounds that are not really present. The patient will sometimes hear multiple voices and the voices can either be talking to the patient or to one another.

These voices that the patient hears can influence them to behave in a particular manner. Researchers at the <u>Mayo Foundation</u> for Medical Education and Research provide the following description: "They [the voices] may make ongoing criticisms of what you're thinking or doing, or make cruel comments about your real or imagined faults.

Voices may also command you to do things that can be harmful to yourself or to others." A patient exhibiting these auditory hallucinations may be observed talking to himself because the person believes that the voices are actually present.

Early diagnosis is important for the successful treatment of schizophrenia

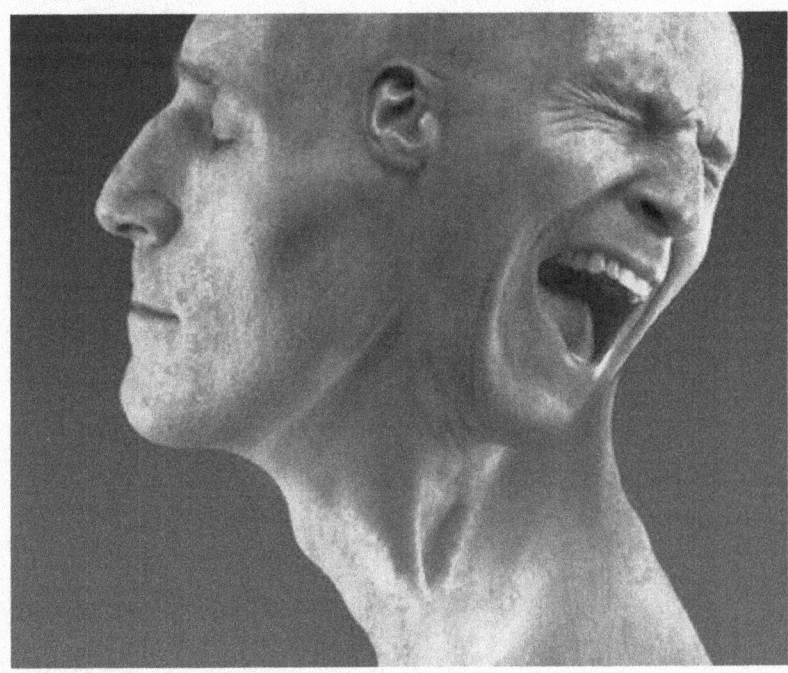

Time for reg to kill

Jack D McVitie (1932, Battersea, London – 29 October 1967, Stoke Newington, London), more commonly known as **Jack the Hat**, was a notorious English criminal from London of the 1950s – 1960s. He is posthumously famous for triggering the imprisonment and downfall of the Kray twins. He had acted as an enforcer and hitman with links to "the firm", and was murdered by Reggie Kray in 1967

McVitie married Marie Marney in Surrey in 1950. The nickname *Jack The Hat* is said to be because of a trilby hat that he wore to cover up his hair loss. A known drug trafficker by the 1960s, he had been an associate of the Kray twins for some time and, although never a permanent member of *The Firm*, was regularly employed to commit various crimes on their behalf.

In 1967 Ronald Kray paid McVitie £500 in advance to kill ex-friend and business partner Leslie Payne, promising he would give another 500 when the job was finished, amid fears that Payne was about to inform the police of his criminal activities. McVitie and a friend, Billy Exley, set off to shoot Payne, but were unsuccessful. Exley, the driver, suffered from heart trouble and McVitie was now heavily dependent on drugs. Exley started to lose his nerve when McVitie produced a handgun, in Exley's words, "the size of a bleedin' cannon."

Arriving at Payne's home, McVitie hammered loudly on the front door, which luckily for Payne was opened by his wife. "He's not in," she said. "That's all right," said McVitie and he and Exley left. Instead of repaying the money McVitie kept it. This incident led, in part, to McVitie's death

On 29 October 1967, McVitie was invited to a party on Evering Road in Stoke Newington, London, with several of his underworld associates and their families. The Krays had secretly arrived at the party first and had spent an hour clearing away guests. Reggie Kray's initial plan to shoot McVitie upon entry failed. His gun jammed and, instead, he stabbed McVitie repeatedly in the face, chest and stomach as part of a brief but violent struggle. The twins quickly fled the scene and McVitie's body was deposited wrapped in aneiderdown and left outside St. Mary's Church, Rotherhithe by Tony and Chris Lambrianou, and Ronnie Bender, who were minor members of the Firm.

When the Krays discovered the whereabouts of the corpse, they ordered it to be immediately moved, probably because of the close proximity of friend and associate Freddie Foreman. The body was never recovered, although in an interview in 2000 (which featured Reg Kray giving a frank account of the activity of The Firm 12 days before his death) Foreman admitted to throwing McVitie's body from a boat into the sea at <u>Newhaven</u>,

Fred Foreman "" Brown bread fred "" armed robber and friend to the krays

This is the house in Evering Road where Reggie Kray stabbed to death, Jack 'the Hat' McVitie

Swinging London in 60 s

Swinging London is a catch-all term applied to the fashion and cultural scene that flourished in London in the 1960s. It consisted largely of music, discotheques, and mod fashion.

Swinging London was a youth-oriented phenomenon that emphasized the new and modern. It was a period of optimism and hedonism, and a cultural revolution. One catalyst was the recovery of the British economy after post-World War II austerity which lasted through much of the 1950s. "Swinging London" was defined by *Time* magazine in its issue of 15 April 1966 and celebrated in the name of the pirate radio station, Swinging Radio England, that began shortly afterward. However, "swinging" in the sense of hip or fashionable had been used since the early 1960s, including by Norman Vaughan in his "swinging/dodgy" patter on *Sunday Night at the London Palladium*. In 1965, Diana Vreeland, editor of *Vogue* magazine, said "London is the most swinging city in the world at the moment." Later that year, the American singer Roger Miller had a hit record with "England Swings", which steps around the progressive youth culture (both musically and lyrically). 1967 saw the release of Peter Whitehead's cult documentary film *Tonite Lets All Make Love in London* which accurately summed up both the culture of Swinging London through celebrity interviews, and the music with its accompanying soundtrack release featuring Pink Floyd.

Already heralded by Colin MacInnes' 1959 novel *Absolute Beginners*, Swinging London was underway by the mid-1960s and included music by The Beatles, The Rolling Stones, The Kinks, The Who, The Small Faces, and other artists from what was known in the United States as the "British Invasion". Psychedelic rock from artists such as The Jimi Hendrix Experience, Pink Floyd, Cream, and Traffic grew significantly in popularity. This sort of music was heard in the United Kingdom over pirate radio stations such as Radio Caroline, Wonderful Radio London, and Swinging Radio England because the BBC did not allow this on their radio station

During the time of Swinging London, fashion and photography were featured in *Queen* magazine, which drew attention to fashion designer Mary Quant.

The model Jean Shrimpton was another icon and one of the world's first supermodels. She was the world's highest paid and most photographed model during this time. Shrimpton was called "The Face of the '60s", in which she has been considered by many as "the symbol of Swinging London" and the "embodiment of the 1960s". Other popular models of the era included Veruschka, Peggy Moffitt, and Penelope Tree. The model Twiggyhas been called "the face of 1966" and "the Queen of Mod," a label she shared with others, such as Cathy McGowan, who hosted the television rock show, *Ready Steady Go!* from 1964 to 1966.

Mod-related fashions such as the miniskirt stimulated fashionable shopping areas such as Carnaby Street and King's Road, Chelsea. The fashion was a symbol of youth culture.[*citation needed*]

The British flag, the Union Jack, became a symbol, assisted by events such as England's home victory in the 1966 World Cup.

The Mini-Cooper car (launched in 1959) was used by a fleet of mini-cab taxis highlighted by advertising that covered their paintwork

The phenomenon was featured in many films of the time. These include *Darling* (1965), *The Knack ...and How to Get It* (1965), the Michelangelo Antonioni film *Blowup* (1966), *Alfie* (1966), *Morgan: A Suitable Case for Treatment* (1966), *Georgy Girl* (1966), *The Jokers* (1967), *Casino Royale* (1967), *Smashing Time* (1967), *To Sir, with Love* (1967), *Bedazzled* (1967), *Poor Cow* (1967), *I'll Never Forget What's'isname* (1967), *Up the Junction*(1968), *Joanna* (1968), *Otley* (1968), *The Magic Christian* (1969), *The Brain* (1969), and *Performance* (1970).

One television series that reflected the spirit of Swinging London was *The Avengers* (1961-1969)

This is the pub the Krays once owned here in 1960

Now

Maureen Flanagan with Chris Lambrianou and 'Legend' movie star Tom Hardy who played both

Who says crime pays? Ronnie Knight is broke and living in sheltered housing...

Ex-husband of Babs Windsor. Gangster king of the Costa del Crooks. Today, Ronnie Knight is broke and living in sheltered housing...

For Ronnie Knight, the worst thing that can happen is for a man to lose face. So when we meet, I'm not too surprised to find he's wearing a pair of handmade Spanish shoes and a white tailored shirt.

He likes to look dapper. That's why Barbara Windsor, his former wife of 22 years, fell for him, he says. 'She said women love to see a man with his shoes and socks on. She told me it's why she fell for me, because I had my suit on.'

That was back in the days when Knight had wads of cash in his bespoke pockets.

The law, which meant you couldn't be tried twice for the same offence, was scrapped on Monday 4 April 2005, after 800 years on the statute book. And that could reopen cases including those of Ronnie Knight, the ex-husband of EastEnders actress Barbara Windsor, and Kray Twins associate Freddie Foreman.Both have written books where they allegedly confess to involvement in murders.

Ronnie Knight,

Freddie Foreman

Ronnie Kray relaxing with a friend at Victoria Park in Hackney, London

Ronnie and Charlie Kray on a day out at the seaside with friends and children

(From left) Johnny Carden, Willie Malone, Joe Schaffer and Pat Connolly at Reggie Kray & Frances Shea's wedding

Charlie Krays Mum and Dad introduce former champion boxer Larry Gains to the horse actor Ronnie Fraser won in a raffle

New Durham Police HQ

Ronnie Kray's record at police HQ

The criminal record of gangster Ronnie Kray has been discovered at a police headquarters following an office move.

In the file he is described as a dog breeder, wardrobe dealer and club owner who will kill in any circumstances.

It also contains three never-been-seen photographs of the London crime boss and under the section "peculiarities" it says his "eyebrows meet over nose".

The document dating back to the 1950s was found at Durham Police HQ, near the prison Kray was sent to in 1969.

The report describes him as being "5ft 7.5ins tall with a fresh complexion, brown eyes and dark brown hair".

The photos in the file, from the then North Eastern Criminal Record Office, are believed to have been taken at Durham Jail.

Kray was sent to the prison after being convicted in March 1969 of murdering George Cornell, who was shot, and Jack "The Hat" McVitie, who was stabbed, in the East End.

He was joined at Durham by his twin brother Reggie and members of their gang.

He would brook no incompetence or interference from anyone

In a stark character assessment, the document said: "Ronald Kray has been the leader of a ruthless and terrible gang for a number of years... he has strong homosexual tendencies and an uncontrollable temper and has been able to generate terror not only in the lesser minions of his gang, but also in the close and trusted members.

"He would brook no incompetence or interference from anyone and was very conscious not only of his own public image but also that of his underlings. "For this reason he used to like to set an example and enjoyed the name of 'the Colonel' amongst his subordinates."

The record starts in October 1950, shortly after Kray's 17th birthday, when he was sentenced to one day in police detention at a juvenile court for attempting to take and drive away a motor car without consent.

It details his later appearances at magistrates' courts on charges of assaulting police and at the Old Bailey where he was accused of wounding with intent and possessing a loaded revolver.

Other court appearances include attempting to bribe a police officer, unlawful gaming, and being found in a common gaming house.

Kray was transferred from Durham to Parkhurst Prison on the Isle of Wight in 1970, and then to Broadmoor, where he died in 1995.

Durham Police said it would be finding a suitable home for the historic criminal file, possibly a museum.

Ronnie Kray here

Married to the Mob: Roberta Kray talks

Notorious gangster Reggie Kray died in a Norwich hotel in October 2000. His wife, Roberta Kray, talks to Look East's Debbie Tubby about his life, death, crimes and punishment.

By the time Reggie Kray lost his battle with bladder cancer in 2000, he and twin brother Ronnie had attained iconic status.
There was no glamour and there was no financial benefit from marrying Reg.

- Roberta Kray

The pair had been jailed for 30 years in 1969 for the murder of fellow gangster Jack "The Hat" McVitie.

The Kray brothers had controlled the most notorious mafia-style criminal gang ever seen in Britain during the 1950s and 1960s

Yet they also had an aura of glamour and celebrity and were frequently photographed with the likes of the then starlet Barbara Windsor.
Home Secretary Jack Straw finally released Reggie in August 2000 because of his deteriorating health.

The campaign for his release had previously failed to win him parole. In 1998 the Parole Board said that he remained a devious and manipulative personality.

After a period in the Norwich and Norfolk Hospital, Reggie chose to end his days at the Beefeater Town House Hotel in Norwich because of its river view.

His wife, Roberta, who married him in prison in 1997 was by his side, and has now written a book - Reggie Kray: A Man Apart - about his life and death.

Roberta Kray is now in dispute with the prison authorities herself over wedding photographs, she says are being withheld.

Reg and Roberta on the wedding day

'council of war' decided Ronnie and Reggie were dangerously out of control and should be "ironed out".

A top Kray associate has revealed how a 'council of war' decided Ronnie and Reggie were dangerously out of control and should be "ironed out".

Freddie Foreman said it was only the fact the twins were arrested and jailed in 1969 that saved their lives.

The former gangster said he had decided action must be taken after he was told by a psychotic Ronnie to dispose of the body of Billy Gentry who was about to be lured into an ambush.

"Billy Gentry was a good fellah," Foreman recalls. "I've done loads of 'bird' with Gentry, so I told Ron to forget about it and calm down. I thought he was raving mad."

That was the turning point. Foreman held his notorious "council of war" at Simpson's in The Strand with some of London's top gang leaders.

"I reported that night back to my pals and said there's only one thing for it," Foreman admits. "I thought the twins should be 'ironed out'.

The two of them should be shot because they were dangerous to everybody. That was my thought and several other people.

"If the twins hadn't been arrested, that's what would have happened. That was on the cards."

Albert Donoghue - Kray Enforcer

Big Albert Donoghue was an integral member of the Kray gang. He was the minder to Reg Kray, being very tough and turned against them when he was expected to take the responsibility for a murder committed by somebody else, but he witnessed. Donoghue was a known young tough and after a friend was badly hurt by the Krays, a remark was reputedly misconstrued and Donoghue was shot in the leg by Reg Kray. Donoghue said nothing to Police and this earned him recruitment to the Kray mob.

Albert Donoghue
Former Kray Gang Member

When Frank "The Mad Axeman" Mitchell escaped from Dartmoor Prison, Donoghue was one who went to take supplies to the house where Mitchell was hiding out. A woman named Lisa was supplied to keep Mitchell happy, but unfortunately, Mitchell, it is said, fell for her. But Mitchell became very restless and wanted to get out and about. Despite his tough reputation, Donoghue knew he would never stop Mitchell, as he had unusually phenomenal strength. The Krays decided that Mitchell was too much trouble, and asked Freddie Foreman to "sort out" the problem. A van arrived with Foreman, Alf Gerrard. When Mitchell climbed into the van, Foreman & Gerrard opened fire, killing Mitchell. They drove off and let Donoghue out later. The problem of the girl, Lisa, was sorted out later. Donoghue took her away from the house, and took her some place where they spent the night together.

Albert Donoghue, Billy Frost, Lenny Hamilton now

When Reg Kray killed Jack McVitie, Donoghue redecorated the room that the murder occurred in. When the arrests went down, Donoghue was expected to take the rap for Mitchell but refused to. He went to the Police. Even the killer of Mitchell, Foreman, said that the Krays put Donoghue in a difficult situation but he handled it badly. Foreman later admitted that the evidence Donoghue gave in court was true. This being the murder of Mitchell. Yet, when you read his memoirs, yes, there are the exaggerations or lies, but he never made excuses for what he did, and made it clear that they were all thugs. Kray ass kisser Tony "Gang Boss" Lambrianou liked to paint Donoghue black as black whilst excusing and justifying the actions of his heroes. "All the men wore three piece suits" said the "Gang Boss". "Yes" said Donoghue "But we were still thugs!" In the case of Lisa, when asked if he would have killed her if ordered to, he said that, yes, eventually he would have. Brutal honesty I call that. He readily admitted he could kill. The "Gang Boss" made much of how violent Donoghue was, whilst conveniently ignoring the violence and murder committed by his heroes.   Donoghue never hid from anybody, staying in his home area. According to a book involving Foreman & Lambrianou, Donoghue received a severe beating late on in his life. Obviously his assailant had to wait until he was old and getting infirm before daring to do something. Does this indicate how dangerous he was? Still able to mix it so we will avoid him until he gets really old? Donoghue was a criminal, a thug who could easily kill, but it made a change to hear somebody say "We were thugs. We would do anything to anybody!"

'Charlie Richardson" Kray rival for london

The church rooftops must have lifted off their eaves in jubilation this week at the death of Charlie Richardson. The Sixties Torture Gang boss made his fortunes as a scrap-metal dealer in Camberwell and he was notorious for taking anything that fell off the back of a lorry at cut-throat prices: 'As God is my witness after I pay you and the Old Bill all I'm left with is a cold.'

Charlie liked God. In Durham Prison's special wing in the late Sixties, when he was serving 25 years for torture and I was serving 26 years for armed robbery, he would always go to church on a Sunday even if he was the only member of the congregatio Charlie fascinated me as he was a lot more than a "rough diamond". He was a one-off. As Wilde noted most people are other people... ("Their thoughts are someone else's opinions, their lives a mimicry, their passions a quotation.") Not Charlie – he was one of the others, his own man. Given that he was ungodly as you could get I once asked him why he went to church. He replied, "It's good for people to believe in God. I like to set an example." Of course, what he meant was the more believers there were, the better the pickings for Charlie. Everything Charlie said or did had to be interpreted for its hidden agenda.

Despite all the grief he gave me, as a people-watcher I still felt blessed by being able to study such a unique person. The point about Charlie was that while anthropologists will go to any lengths to study tribes untouched by civilisation he had far more of his share of what civilisation had to offer and still been untouched by it.

He was a good judge of character –especially when it came to spotting people's weaknesses. He was talking one day about how he booked a person. He said: "I just ask myself if they wanted to borrow a hundred quid how much I'd lend them." I couldn't resist, so I asked him how much he'd lend me. "Well, John, don't be offended, but nothing 'cos you're always in prison, so I'd never get my money back."

Charlie never coughed to anything, even though he was habitually up to everything. Even if you had him bang to rights on something, he would swear on his kids' eyesight that it wasn't down to him. This was a favourite oath of his: the fact that he had a myriad of offspring doubtless with 20-20 vision by a multiplicity of women was also pure Charlie. Even to people who knew the real griff he would say all the evidence brought against him at his 1966 trial was, "cooked up...something out of a storybook"

When he sentenced him Mr Justice Lawton said: "One is ashamed to think that one lives in a society that contained men like you. You are vicious, sadistic and a disgrace to civilisation."

Lawton, whose father had been a prison warder, did the media rounds after he retired and in the Eighties I occasionally met him in the green room after we'd crossed swords over some legal issue. At one of these I reminded him of his sentencing remarks to Charlie Richardson. I told him, "You were right. The only thing you were wrong about – and that was beyond your powers – is you didn't sentence him be tortured." He was taken aback. "You knew him, obviously. Was he that bad?" I replied. "Worse. Charlie is evil... in the nicest possible way. Evil people sometimes are."

I knew how bad Charlie was because I became a close friend of Roy Hall who was also convicted at the Torture Gang trial. He was sentenced to 10 years. Roy manned the generator that was used to torture Charlie's victims. It was a hand-cranked generator that was for sending out SOS signals from aircraft ; Charlie had taken it from a scrapped WWII bomber they'd cut up at his Camberwell yard in New Church Road. One afternoon in Durham's special wing Roy and I were idly watching an old movie on TV, which portrayed Odette Churchill withstanding electric shock torture

Gangster Charlie Richardson became infamous for his use of torture

Roy commented: "That bollocks. It's impossible." I reflexively demurred as I am by nature contrary and I pointed out that scientifically women withstand pain better than men. "What you on about John? Don't forget I know." I looked puzzled. "I was with Charlie, remember... When you put people under the electrodes they go. They tell you everything."

 asked the obvious question that even when people supposedly confess how do you know they are not lying. "Yeah, people lie because you want stuff that they don't want to tell you," Roy said. "But you know that, so you push it to when they have to tell the truth, when they can't do anything else." I looked puzzled.

I "They can't take it anymore. No one can. They turn into little kids and ask for 'Mummy'. It's something you have to see to know. But they can't lie to you. Even months later if you go into a pub 'cos you have to talk to them, they go back into it. They're broken and it never mends."

I felt the cold, clammy clutch of something horrible... evil. In a way to torture someone is worse than to kill them. When you break a person's humanity and personality like this, they are no more than the living dead, except they have to live it for the rest of their lives. I didn't look at Ray. I just kept watching the movie.

His confession – in a way that was what it was – dried up and we never spoke about it again. But for all my fascination with Charlie's often comical antics in prison I now looked at him in a different light. Charlie was the force majeure of what went on at his scrap-metal yard in the 60s. It would not have happened if he hadn't been what he was.

Outsiders often think prisons are full of evil people. They're not. There are a lot of bad people locked up but most are bad in a conventional way. They just do what those around them do; they mimic what the people they have fell in with do. Evil people are probably as rare as truly saintly people; I don't know. But as far as my thoughts about Charlie Richardson go I am with the church rooftops.

John McVicar

A gangster, armed robber and serial prison escape artist, named "public enemy No 1" in the Sixties, McVicar went straight in the Seventies, took a degree and became a writer.

John McVicar

Ronnie Kray. Boxer, **gangst**er, mad man – but poet?

"everything at peace in the valley,
and on the hill,
everything so quiet and still,
breathe in the country air and look at the beauty,
all around,
only god can grant us this peace to be found."

"Dear God, do I speak in vain?
can no one hear me when
the feelings of my heart are in pain
I am weak. I am strong. I am vain.
But all I want is the peace of mind that one gets
Going down a country lane"

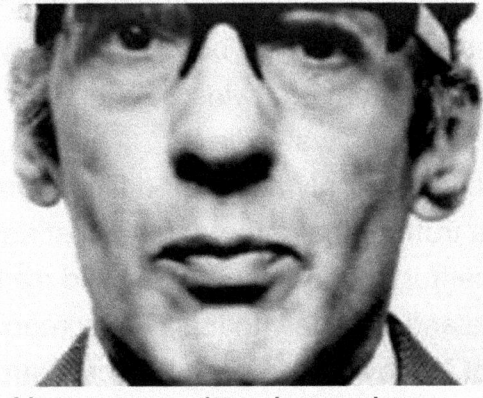

Above was written by ron kray

Flashy suits, fancy clubs and Freudian fights: a new film about Ronnie and Reggie Kray polishes their brutal myth into a glossy true-crime thriller. Legend director Brian Helgeland on getting under the skin of the notorious East End gangsters and shooting two Tom Hardys

Brian Helgeland first heard of the Kray twins in 1998, when the writer-director met a veteran English showbusiness manager with a dramatic scar. Eventually, curiosity nudged him into asking how it happened. *That*, he was told, had been the Krays. The bloodcurdling story involved would work its way into the script when, years later, Helgeland was making Legend, a new film about the brothers. Soon afterwards, a letter arrived from the manager's lawyer.

"It said, 'First off, none of that ever happened. Second, if you put it in the movie, we will sue you.' Then it said he didn't even remember meeting me." Puzzled, Helgeland dug back into the original story; he realised his source had been in prison when he claimed to have met the twins. "So the very first thing I heard about them was a lie."

This much seems only fitting for a film about the Krays, the truth of their story forever lost somewhere in a half-century of hearsay and tabloid exclusives. And Helgeland was new to it all. On screen, Legend is filled not just by the presence of Tom Hardy – who plays both Reggie and Ronnie – but by London and its folklore.

In person, its maker is a crewcut man of 54 from Providence, Rhode Island, in crumpled beige chinos, who had, until recently, never set foot in the East End. Matching Helgeland to the Krays was the idea of Working Title, the muscular London production company. The logic was straightforward. The screenplay Helgeland wrote for the company's Iraq war thriller Green Zone was well regarded; further back in his career had been the script for Clint Eastwood's acclaimedMystic River and an Oscar for writing LA Confidential, each dark-eyed tales of men, crime and violence. As a director, he had got good reviews for 42, a recent biopic of the African American baseball pioneer Jackie Robinson.

His nationality never gave him pause. He took the job, collected up the vast weight of Krays literature – including Reg Kray's Book of Slang, published from Parkhurst prison in 1989 – and decamped to London. There he met surviving henchmen and acquaintances including Barbara Windsor, former gangster Freddie Foreman and Maureen Flanagan, hairdresser to the Krays' mother Violet.

Between the books and the old pals, the chaos almost defeated him. On the one hand were the endless stories of rough-hewn Robin Hoods helping Bethnal Green grannies across the road. On the other were the accounts of sadism and psychosis. "The truth about them seemed very elusive, and the more I researched it the more I thought 'You know, I don't know if I really do want to make a movie about these guys.' Because I couldn't figure them out."

He watched the other film version of the brothers' story, 1990's The Krays, starring Spandau Ballet's Gary and Martin Kemp and a ferocious Billie Whitelaw as Violet. It didn't help. "The matriarchal stuff in there was great. But they did that. I had to do something else."

In the end, the something else was Frances Shea. The unhappy bride of Reg (played by Australian actress Emily Browning), married for eight weeks in 1965 and a suicide by 1967, Shea gave Helgeland his angle. Legend would be a true-crime Romeo and Juliet, young love poisoned by the malign influence of Ron – here flamboyantly unhinged – and Reg's demons too. Yet for much of the film Reg is quite the catch, a gleaming slab of charm in tailored suit and tiepin, strutting out of his Mum's to a soundtrack of Booker T's Green Onions.

Legend goes big on 60s glitz with the sheen of men's magazines. Is Helgeland worried he over-did it? "I know that's where the film lives or dies. But they were glamorous guys. Everyone says, 'Oh, the Richardsons were a tougher gang'. But David Bailey didn't want to photograph the Richardsons. The Richardsons weren't hanging out with movie stars. Gangsters are glamorous on some level. I didn't invent the glamour that goes with them."

Helgeland's career began with horror movies (his first screenplay credit was A Nightmare on Elm Street 4: the Dream Master). But he talks with an enthusiast's knowledge about gangsters, how the Krays compare to American examples such as Bugsy Siegel and Meyer Lansky. He says the ethics of portraying such men had to be weighed alongside the job at hand. "They're the heroes of the film. I want to be on the ground with them, rather than looking down and judging them. I don't think I'm looking *up* at them or saying they didn't do what they did, but you have to be on the side of your protagonists."

With fact and fiction so eternally mixed up, the film's title sets the tone. Wading through his library, Helgeland arranged events into timelines to find points of consensus. From there, he applied what might be called scriptwriter's licence: peppering the landmark facts – the murders of George Cornell and Jack McVitie, the tabloid sex scandal involving peer Lord Boothby – with more speculative set-pieces such as Reg shinning up Frances's drainpipe with a ring and Ron parading in a silk scarf with a donkey. "Grounded in reality," Helgeland says of his approach. "I didn't want to invent too much." He says of one pivotal moment: "if it's not true, then it should be."

Getting the dialogue right was a matter of personal pride, but even with Reg Kray's Book of Slang it fell to Hardy to change a reference to Betty Crocker into England's own Fanny Cradock. (Sticklers may still wince as Ron recalls a sexual encounter leaving the other party "like a pretzel".) With its insistent voiceover from Browning, the sense is that Legend was made for America. Helgeland shakes his head: "No, no. It was definitely made for the UK."

Helgeland alighted on Hardy as his star not after seeing his singular turn in prison head-trip Bronson, but the low-key boxing drama Warrior. This, he thought, was his Reg. With Working Title just as keen, a dinner was arranged to sound out their quarry. "And all he talked about was Ron. Afterwards, he said 'I want to do it but only if I can play Ron as well.'"

To Helgeland luring Hardy into playing the matinee idol is a coup. "We get Tom as the groomed leading man everyone wants him as – but he's never let himself be before – because his side of the deal is getting to play Ron."

He says his preference had always been for one actor to take both roles, avoiding the parlour game of finding two male leads who could pass for twins. "And actors always get competitive." But while visual effects can do remarkable things, he realised the basic technology of splicing together split screens hadn't changed since Hayley Mills played identical twins in 1961's The Parent Trap. He began to brood. "I looked at films with one actor playing twins, but I'd get depressed because you were always so aware of what they were doing, and by that time I was committed to it. I'd think 'This is not going to work.'"

In fact, Hardy's charisma is all you notice. There is, inevitably, a brawl between the brothers, staged in their nightclub Esmeralda's Barn with an eye-catching degree of violence; Freudian viewers can soon unpick the sight of one Tom Hardyendangering the testicles of another. That same tone pervades the film: Greek tragedy in expensive suits with a large dash of slapstick.

"I'm a big believer that any scene can be goofy and poignant at the same time. But it's a challenge to make it work. When we were filming you could tell people were looking at us like, 'What are they doing? This is just silly.' But you know, in the editing room, we would grind off the stuff that was too funny, or that crossed the line." On set, Hardy was encouraged to ad lib. "He had to have the freedom to do that. To get it right, he had to …" Get it wrong? "Right."

Helgeland ponders what the Krays themselves would make of his film. "Well, I think Reggie would say 'Fair enough. That's how it was.'" And Ron? "I think Ron would enjoy the fact that Tom Hardy was playing him. So yeah, all told, they would dig it."

"""The Krays were glamorous guys"""

Ronnie Kray was a predatory homosexual who terrified young men in Soho in the 1960s so much they hid when they knew he was coming.

According to legendary singer and actor Jess Conrad, who knew the Kray twins well, good looking young men used to vanish for fear of catching Ronnie's eye and being invited back to "a party".

He said: "You had to keep your wits about you if you were a young man and Ronnie really fancied you.

"Word used to go out that the Krays were on their way to a certain pub and all the good looking boys used to pi** off.

"Because otherwise if he asked you to go back to the house you had to go back and that was it.

"You'd make yourself scarce, unless you didn't want to make yourself scarce of course."

t's always been known Ronnie Kray was gay with a fondness for violence but Jess' recollection is one of the few accounts of how he exerted power for sexual ends. Jess, who had a string of chart hits and stared in films and in West End stage shows such as Joseph, also said he believes the violent twins Ronnie and Reggie acted on behalf of stars like Diana Dors and Barbara Windsor if men were showing them unwanted attention.

He said: "Just like we liked being around The Krays they loved being around celebrities.

"Dors and Babs (Barbara Windsor) used to love tough guys and so they mixed in the same circles."

Jess said: "I think they also felt that if anyone took a liberty with them because they knew the Krays the bloke would get sorted out.

"I am sure if Dors said she was having trouble with a man they would sort him out.

"Back then the gangsters had great morality, they would never swear in front of wives or girlfriends, they were very respectful of their mothers because of the role they they had played during the war.

"You never pinched another man's wife or mistress, there was a strict code of good marriage.

"There was a Robin Hood thing about them, that they only got involved with other gangsters."

Jess said many men, including himself, were in awe of the gangsters and the way they dressed and carried themselves and were attracted to them.

He said: "You have to remember their time was after the horror of the war and London had been an awful state.

"The only glamour was on the cinema screen and that was people like James Cagney, Edward G Robinson and their gangster films.

"The Krays and the Richardsons had great suits and always had attractive blondes with them and I was attracted to that image.

"Us teenage boys seeing the Krays dressed like they did was like seeing Spencer Tracy.

"We used to want to get near them, find out where they drank, who made their suits, what brand of cigarettes they smoked.

"We wanted to walk like them and find out how they ticked."

Jess, now 79, first came across the twins when he was "spiv" in London in the 1960s before he made it big in show-business.

He said: "We used to hang out in Soho at a club called Sissy Jacksons.

"Back then no-one knew anyone in show business so you hung out with glamorous gangsters like the Krays.

"When they walked in it was like a film star had walked in."

But it was only when he became involved with screen siren Dors, who mixed with tough guys, that he met the Krays and went to parties they were at.

Once he started to be successful in show-business and became friends with other stars he saw them regularly. He said: "They would come to Dors' parties at her house and have a drink and smoke and listen to records.

"People have said her parties were racy but they were nothing by today's standards."

"A big car driven by Ronnie's friend Joey Pyle picked me up and took me to Broadmoor.

"It was surreal, Ronnie spoke very slowly 'would you like a cup of tea', he had time all the time, time to talk.

"He told me he thought I had a great body and asked me if I went running and I told him I did and asked him if he did.

"He told me he did and I then I put my foot in it.

"I looked out the window at the grass and beyond it and said 'around that grass?' and he said 'no, around this room', I thought 'of course not he's locked up'.

"He said the reason he had asked me down is because he wanted me to do a show and said 'money is no object'.

"I thought to myself 'I know Johnny Cash did this but I'm a women's' act'.

"It was a time when I wore a white catsuit and Gary Glitter boots with a jock strap and my wedding tackle well on display and loads of medallions and was an act for teenyboppers.

"This was before CDs of course so I took my band with me and they were as petrified as I was."

Still the gig went ahead and Jess recalls: "I went out in front of 75 inmates – goodness knows what some of them had done - in my cat-suit and did "Johnny B. Goode" with a big finish and there was nothing from them.

"Then Ron went 'yeah' and they all started clapping, and off we went for a hour or whatever and he started the applause off at the end of every number.

"At the end I got a standing ovation, £5,000 which was enough not to work for the rest of the year and a thank you letter from Ronnie.

"I thought it was very funny to think that as a boy if I hadn't got into show-business I might have ended up as a criminal in prison and I ended up doing a gig there."

Handsome: Jess Conrad performed a secret gig in Broadmoor Hospital

Reggie Kray and me, by the woman who made the notorious gangland killer a Christian

He was the gangland boss who ruled the East End with fear and brutal violence.

She was a deeply religious nursery nurse and the daughter of a policeman.

Yet despite their differences, an unlikely friendship formed between Reggie Kray and Carol-Ann Kelly ... and led to the notorious killer renouncing his past and declaring himself a born-again Christian.

During prison visits in the 1980s, Miss Kelly regularly read the Bible with Kray, recalling that his favourite passage was the story of the Crucifixion – when Jesus told the penitent thief on a cross beside him that they would meet in Paradise.

The prison visitor: Miss Kelly with letters she received from gangland boss Kray

In letters never before seen in public, the gangster started writing in 1983 to the devout mother, saying she had helped him find God.

'I became a born again Christian on behalf of you.' he wrote. 'You have played a big part in my life.'

So fond was Kray of the then-married Miss Kelly and her young son David that he paid the rent on a flat on the Isle of Wight so they could visit him at Parkhurst Prison.

She went on to see him once a month until 1989, as well as talking to him over the phone once a fortnight. They eventually lost touch after she travelled to Rwanda to work as a volunteer at an orphanage.

Kray's later claims to have found religion were seen by many as a ruse to curry favour with the authorities and secure his release from jail. But the letters to Miss Kelly suggest he meant what he said.

The friendship began after a chance meeting in 1983, while Miss Kelly was visiting a relative in prison. The pair, who had both been diagnosed with cancer, soon bonded over their respective battles with the disease.

'I became a sort of wife figure to him I suppose, but we were just friends,' said Miss Kelly, now a grandmother in her 50s and living in West Hampstead, north London. 'I saw my role as giving him spiritual help.

'We talked a lot about the cancer, and I tried to get him to understand that he could be set free in prison and use the rest of his life to help others. I couldn't believe it when he told me he prayed for me. To think of a murderer praying is a powerful thing.'

Miss Kelly recovered from cervical cancer in 1987 but Kray's bladder cancer eventually claimed his life in 2000.

The only previous mention of their friendship was in Kray's autobiography A Way of Life, where he wrote:

'Due to Carol's illness I was very concerned. I was so worried about it all that on one particular night I said what was quite a strange prayer.

'I offered myself to God and Jesus Christ as a born again Christian if in turn Carol could be cured.'

Throughout the 80s, the pair exchanged dozens of letters, with Kray thanking Miss Kelly and her family for helping him find God.

He also revealed his frustrations with the parole board over restrictions which stopped him seeing his twin brother Ronnie, and paranoia about his representation by the national press.

He kept a wedding photo of Miss Kelly in his cell, and referred to it in a note saying: 'I still have the wedding photos but they are not for show. I keep them personal,' before signing off 'God Bless, your friend Reg Kray'.

Demonstrating a softer side, the ruthless killer also sent two childlike drawings to Miss Kelly – one of a boxer and one of a Mexican bandit.

In one of his letters – scrawled in his distinctly messy handwriting – he wrote to Miss Kelly encouraging her to remain strong despite her illness and marital problems.

'You must never contemplate suicide. It would be like turning traitor on young David and your mother too.'

He added: 'You need to get your head together for little David.'

Kray also showered the then eight-year-old David with affection, writing: 'Please tell David thanks for his drawing which was good.

'Tell him to dare to dream. If he gets any ideas during his life to put them into practice even if others don't like the ideas as he will eventually see his ideas bare (sic) fruit with a little luck.'

The Kray twins were jailed for life in 1969 for the murder of Jack 'The Hat' McVitie and Ronnie Kray's fatal shooting of George Cornell.

Ronnie died in 1995 at Broadmoor. Reggie was released on compassionate grounds in 2000 and died a month later.

Now a volunteer at Holloway Prison in north London, Miss Kelly intends to auction her Kray letters next year. The proceeds will benefit the Royal Free Hospital in Hampstead.

Rare photograph of a young Ronald "Ronnie" & Reginald "Reggie" Kray. Date & location unknown. Ronald on the left, Reginald on the right.

Reggie and adopted son Brad Kray

What are Twins

Twins are two offspring produced by the same pregnancy. Twins can either be *monozygotic* ("identical"), meaning that they can develop from just one zygote that will then split and form two embryos, or *dizygotic* ("fraternal"), meaning that they can develop from two different eggs; each are fertilized by separate sperm cells.

In contrast, a fetus which develops alone in the womb is called a *singleton*, and the general term for one offspring of a multiple birth is *multiple*.

The human twin birth rate in the United States rose 76% from 1980 through 2009, from 18.9 to 33.3 per 1,000 births. The Yoruba have the highest rate of twinning in the world, at 45–50 twin sets (or 90–100 twins) per 1,000 live births, possibly because of high consumption of a specific type of yam containing a natural phytoestrogen which may stimulate the ovaries to release an egg from each side.

In Central Africa there are 18–30 twin sets (or 36–60 twins) per 1,000 live births. In Latin America, South Asia, and Southeast Asia, the lowest rates are found; only 6 to 9 twin sets per 1,000 live births. North America and Europe have intermediate rates of 9 to 16 twin sets per 1,000 live births.

Multiple pregnancies are much less likely to carry to full term than single births, with twin pregnancies lasting on average 37 weeks, three weeks less than full term.Women who have a family history of fraternal twins have a higher chance of producing fraternal twins themselves, as there is a genetically linked tendency to hyper-<u>ovulate</u>. There is no known genetic link for identical twinning. Other factors that increase the odds of having fraternal twins include maternal age, fertility drugs and other fertility treatments, nutrition, and prior births

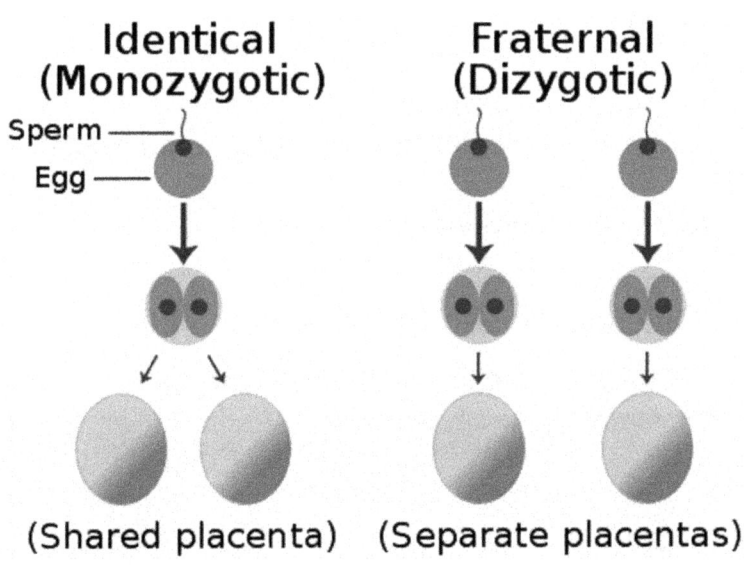

Quirky FACTS

Ronnie Kray first time in a staigthjacket
christmas day 1957

Ronnie Shoots his 1st man
in autumn 1956 a car dealer asked ronnie for
protection from a customer demanding money
after a brief stuggle the customer was shot.

Ronnie starred as a extra in a film cast movie is
called (magic box)

black musem houses murder weapon as a trophy
9mm mauser semi automatic used by ron to kill
cornell

christmas day wedding
charlie kray older brother married dorothy moore

Vision both twins was short sighted

Officially closed to the public: The
Scotland Yard Crime Museum

Tools of the Trade

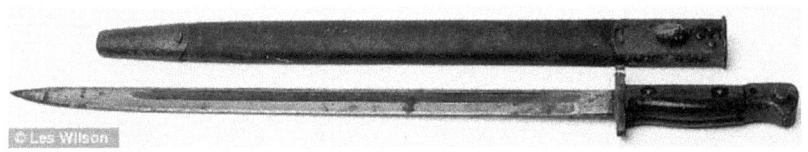

Tool up: Ronnie collected - and used - bayonets, above once owned and used by ron kray

Ronnie Kray's knuckleduster

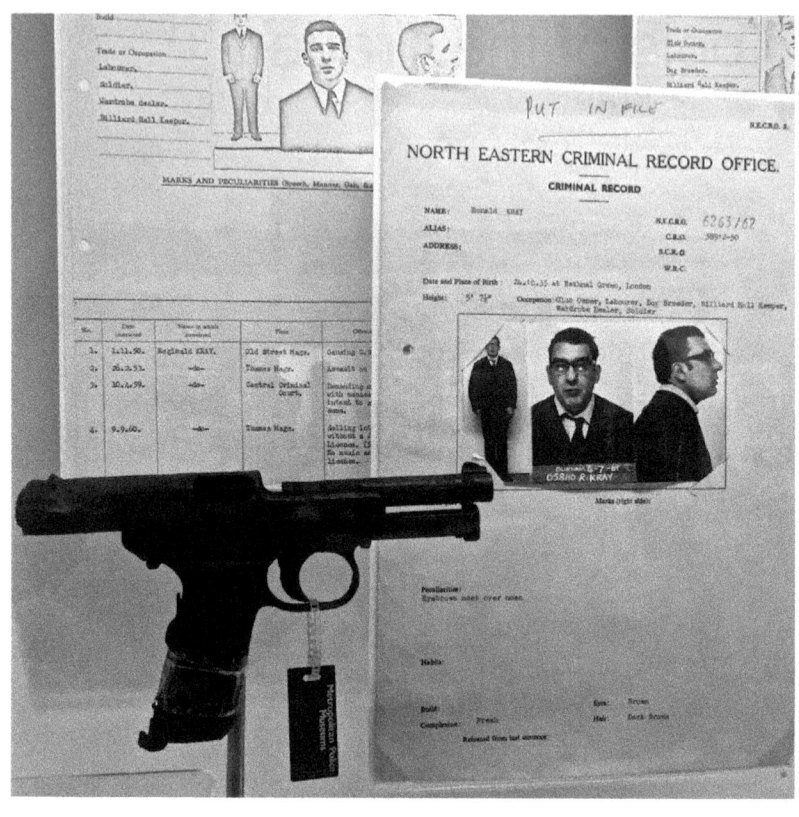

A handgun used by notorious London gangster Ronald Kray

Ronnie's crossbow

Ronnie and Reggie Kray's briefcase with
syringe and posion

Ronnie's cosh - a thick, heavy bar
used as a weapon

One of the Krays owned a catapult

Cigarette Case Ronnie Kray Crop
used for the cigrarette punch

Reggie Kray's penknife

Ronnie's sawn-off shotgun

Reggie's bayonet

Reggie was supposed to kill Jack McVitie with this gun but it jammed leaving him to a much worse fate

Reg (left) Ron at home after the murder of cornell

The twins' passports

CHARLIE KRAY'S PASSPORT

Mad' Frankie Fraser: original hardman who loved to cause panic

When "Mad" Frankie Fraser, who has died after a long life of mayhem, used to be transported in handcuffs from prison to prison, he had a little game he liked to play. As the car in which he was being moved slowed down at traffic lights he would glance out of the window and, if there was a car next to his driven by a couple of young men, he would gesture at them and mouth the words "not yet, not yet" – starting a panic among his escorts.

Panic was what Fraser could cause all too easily. He was one of the orginal razor-slashing hardmen, both feared and fearless. When, in the 1960s, he threw in his lot with the Richardson gang in south London, one fellow villain remarked that it was like China getting the atom bomb. Fraser himself made his choice of gang for very pragmatic reasons. Interviewed for the BBC's Underworld series in 1994, he said: "Using racing terms there would be no race, comparing the Richardsons and the Krays. The Richardsons were miles in front, brain power, everything."

He was the Little Big Man – all five 5ft 5in of him – of the London underworld.

He had seen crime move from the race tracks of Brighton to the bloody Soho feuds of Billy Hill and Jack "Spot" Comer to the present day when, until his health failed over the past few years, he was taking tourists on visits to famous gangland sites and entertaining guests with after-dinner jests about his dark past.

He used to complain that he started life at a great disadvantage because his parents were both honest and hardworking so he had to make his way as a career criminal entirely under his own steam. As he put it: "My mother and father were dead straight so I had to make my own way. If you've got parents who have been to prison they can help you considerably with their contacts."

He started young. As an eight-year-old, without his parents' knowledge, he was working for a gang "on the bucket" at the race tracks, which meant he offered to sponge down the boards for the bookies – a veiled protection racket which made him 7s and 6d a day at a time when his honest dad was making £2.10s a week. "I thought to myself – this is the game to be in," he said later. And that was the game he stayed in until almost his dying day. He was even back in the news last year for having received an asbo. According to one version of the story he had threatened a fellow resident of his south London care home for sitting in his favourite seat. It got him a mention in a House of Commons debate.

Fraser achieved his "mad" soubriquet during the second world war when he managed to get himself out of military service by pretending to be two mailbags short of a heist: to prove his unsuitability he assaulted a doctor and jumped out of the window at the Bradford assessment centre where he had been sent. Crime is one of the few careers where being known as mad is an advantage and over the next 40 years or so Fraser played it to the hilt. He did well in the war, profiting from the lack of able-bodied policemen and the temptations of loot from the blitz. In 1956 he took part in an assault on Comer, one of the would-be kings of Soho, setting about him with a shillelagh. He said afterwards that he would cheerfully have killed him and would have liked to have carved noughts and crosses on his face with a razor to humiliate him. "Unfortunately, there wasn't that amount of time," he remarked later.

Fraser was jailed for seven years for this assault despite his counsel's plea that he was "a weaker vessel of mankind who has been used for a foul purpose". The judge was unimpressed. He was to spend a total of more than 40 years of his life behind bars, in different stretches, often for violence committed in prison. He was a rebel in jail, taking part in whatever riots presented themselves, most notably in the 1969 Parkhurst riot that added more years to his time inside. Jail did not bother him, he said, because he was familiar with it from Jimmy Cagney films and it seemed "quite comfy".

In 1966 he was in court following the murder of Dickie Hart in Mr Smiths' club in south London, but it was the so-called "torture trial" in 1967 when grim tales of violence meted out to those who had fallen foul of the Richardsons emerged. Fraser was accused of pulling out the teeth of his victims with pliers. He joked later that "he gave me good due as a dentist, said it was absolutely painless". Fraser was jailed for 10 years and it was only when he finally emerged that he decided he could spend a bit more time with his family. Even then, trouble seemed to follow him. He was shot in the head outside Turnmills nightclub in Clerkenwell, central London, in 1992. He survived and the apocryphal tale at the time was that the police had asked him what his name was and he replied: "Tutenkham – I'm keeping mum."

Frankie Fraser with girlfriend Marilyn Wisbey – daughter of the Great Train Robber Tom Wisbey

Billy Hill (gangster)

Hill was born into a London criminal family and committed his first stabbing at age fourteen.[1] He began as a house burglar in the late 1920s and then specialized in "smash-and-grab" raids targeting furriers and jewellers in the 1930s.

During World War II, he moved into the black market, specializing in foods and petrol. He also supplied forged documents for deserting servicemen and was involved in West End protection rackets with fellow gangster Jack Spot. In the late 1940s, he was charged with burgling a warehouse and fled to South Africa. Following an arrest there for assault, he was extradited back to Britain, where he was convicted for the warehouse robbery and served time in prison. This was his last jail term. After his release he met Gypsy Riley, better known as "Gyp Hill", who became his common-law wife.[citation needed]

In 1952, he planned the Eastcastle St. postal van robbery netting £287,000 (*2010: £6,440,000*),[2] and in 1954 he organised a £40,000 bullion heist. No one was ever convicted for these robberies. He also ran smuggling operations from Morocco during this period. In 1955, Hill wrote his memoir *Boss of Britain's Underworld*. In it he described his use of the shiv:

I was always careful to draw my knife down on the face, never across or upwards. Always down. So that if the knife slips you don't cut an artery. After all, chivving is chivving, but cutting an artery is usually murder. Only mugs do murder.

Hill was mentor to twins <u>Ronnie and Reggie Kray</u>, advising them in their early criminal careers.

Hill's sister, Maggie Hughes, was one of the <u>Forty Elephants</u> gang of specialist shoplifters. Her story is revealed in *Alice Diamond and the Forty Elephants* by Brian McDonald.

In late 1956 Home Secretary Gwilym Lloyd George authorised the tapping of Hill's phone. At the time gang warfare had broken out in London between Hill and erstwhile partner in crime, Jack Spot. In 1956, Spot and wife Rita were attacked by Hill's bodyguard,Frankie Fraser, Bobby Warren and at least half a dozen other men. Both Fraser and Warren were given seven years for their acts of violence.

The Bar Council approached the police and requested the tapes in order to provide evidence for an investigation into the professional conduct of Hill's barrister, Patrick Marrinan. Sir Frank Newsam, Permanent Secretary at the Home Office, allowed them access.When this use of tapping powers was revealed to Parliament in June 1957, Leader of the Opposition Hugh Gaitskell demanded a full explanation. Rab Butler pledged that it would not be a precedent and that he would consider withdrawing the evidence and asking the Bar council to disregard it.

In the 1960s Hill was busy fleecing aristocrats at card tables. In Douglas Thompson's book *The Hustlers*, and the subsequent documentary on Channel 4, *The Real Casino Royale*, the club's former financial director John Burke and Hill's associate Bobby McKew,claimed that John Aspinall worked with Hill to cheat the players at the Clermont Club.Some of the wealthiest people in Britain were swindled out of millions of pounds, thanks to a gambling con known as 'the Big Edge'.

Marked cards could be discovered too easily; instead the low cards were slightly bent across their width in a small mangle before being repackaged. High cards were slightly bent lengthwise.Hill's Card sharks were introduced to the tables by Aspinall; they could read whether a card was high, low or an unbent zero card (10 to king) thus gaining a 60-40 edge. The final stage involved "skimming" the profits from the table to avoid attention. On the first night of the operation, the tax-free winnings for the house were £14,000 (*2007: £280,000*). According to McKew the 18th Earl of Derby lost £40,000 (*2014: £590,000*) in one night.

The club's former financial director John Burke quit in late 1965, a year into the scam. He had been tipped off about an investigation but Aspinall was determined to carry on. However Aspinall no longer had someone to deal with "the dirty end" of the operation. After two years' operation the Big Edge was closed. Hill respected Aspinall's decision and the partnership dissolved

Hill retired from crime in the 1970s and died on 1 January 1984, aged 72

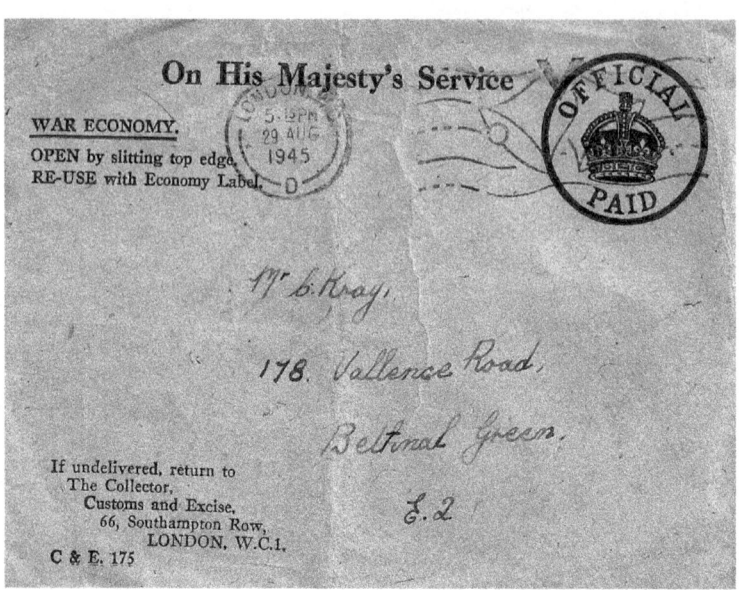

taxman sent to Mr.C.Kray at 178 Vallance Road in 1945 while the war was still going on.

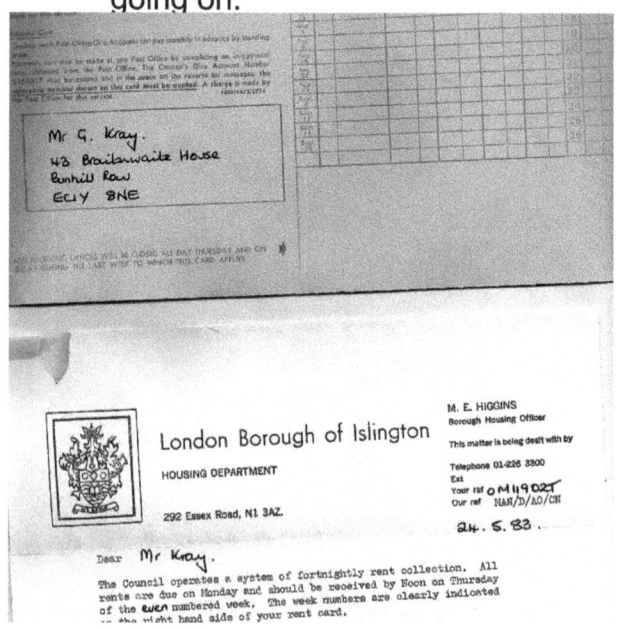

Kray family rent book

Joe Louis
c/o Caesars Palace
Las Vegas, Nevada
U.S.A. - 4 O...

Dear Ronnie & Reggy,
Your brother Charlie told me what your address was, and I wanted to write to you for quite awhile, but didn't know your address. I sure hope that both of you are getting along as good as possible. I hope their is some way you could make it out in the near future. If I get to England I'll come visit you. Stay well,
your friend,

Jo Louis

1944

fax sent to the twins by JOE LOUIS one of the greatest heavyweights ever.

151

(From left) Teddy Smith, Micky Fawcett, Johnny Davis, Reggie Kray, Freddie Mills, Ronnie Kray, Dicky Morgan and Sammy Lederman at Freddie Mills' Nite Spot.

Eddie Pucci (Frank Sinatras Bodyguard), Ronnie Kray, George Raft, Reggie Kray, Rocky Marciano and Charlie Kray (Older Brother of the Kray Twins)

Tony Burns with Reggie Kray in 1997.

Reggie Kray (left) winks at the press as he and his brothers, Charlie and Ronnie, arrive at the Old Bailey. 4 March, 1969

Reggie Kray, Rocky Marciano, George Raft,
Charles and Ronnie Kray ...

Reggie Kray at the El Morocco club in Gerrard St,
Violet and Frances Kray are on the right

How an arts-loving schoolgirl so beautiful she was mistaken for Brigitte Bardot ended her life as the tragic first Mrs Reggie Kray

She was beautiful, intelligent and innocent. Yet while growing up in the fifties in London's east End, neither she nor Frances Shea's family could ever have imagined that her entire life would be tragically destroyed because she caught Reggie Kray's eye when she was just a teenager.

despite there being so much said, written, scripted, documented and delivered to the public gaze about the Kray twins, little has been told or revealed about Frances Shea, briefly at the centre of it all.

In 1965, Frances had married Reggie Kray in a blaze of tabloid publicity, but left him after a matter of weeks - and killed herself just over two years after the marriage.

Even close to half a century on from her suicide at the age of 23, total strangers flock to her grave, place flowers and ponder the power of her beauty. Mostly, though, they wonder about the tragedy of her short existence.

Frances Shea was no criminal. She wasn't a cynical gangster's moll with one eye on the main chance, drawn in by the easy money, the flash nightclubs and the sparkle of celebrity. She was a beautiful innocent, which was precisely why Reggie was so drawn to her.

Wherever his sexual tastes lay up to that point, whatever the complexity of his relationship with Ronnie or his crimes, there seems little doubt that the minute Reggie saw the pretty auburn-haired teenager with the big eyes, he experience something of a shock. It is what the French call 'le coup de foudre', a bolt of lightning - which some describe as love at first sight.

Very soon, he'd introduced Frances to his family in Vallance Road. The twins' cousin Rita liked the young girl immediately.

'She had shorter, quite dark hair then. Very pretty girl. Big brown eyes. She was quite shy, quite an innocent really - as you are at that age. But intelligent, you could see that,' recalled Rita.

During their 'honeymoon' period in 1960, Reggie took to meeting Frances outside her office in the Strand after she'd finished work. They'd go to the movies. There were drives out to the country. On other occasions, he'd take her 'up West' to places like the Astor Club, a swish nightclub off Berkeley Square in Mayfair.

rare pic of Reg Krays first wife Francis.

Proudly, Reggie showed everyone the photos he'd taken with Frances in the Astor club, the first of many photos of the couple in a glamorous setting.

'She looks like Brigitte Bardot', said his friend Danny. Reggie was chuffed. His girl looked like a French movie star - yet she was from the mean streets of the East End, just like him. She was his trophy.

But soon, Reggie was back in prison. While the separation from Frances turned out to be really painful for him, her everyday life went on.

Two years after the marriage, Frances had killed herself through a drugs overdose

Correspondence from that time reveals the truth of Reggie's obsession with Frances. But Frances's own responses were mature and clear thinking, given her age. Her writings revealed a very different girl to the compliant 'arm candy' previously portrayed.

After his release, their relationship continued. But despite plans to marry, Frances continually stalled on their wedding plans. Along with the trouble she sensed whenever Reggie was with his brother Ronnie, Frances was starting to see for herself where her place was within the twins' world: a pampered doll, controlled by an intense, possessive man who wanted her to be influenced by only himself.

Yet, socially, as far as other people were concerned, she was a no-go area: Reggie's property.

Rows between them started to be a regular occurrence. They usually began when they were on their way home from a night out or after she'd spent an evening in the kitchen at Vallance Road, waiting for Reg to come home.

That was her life: waiting for Reg to finish whatever it was. It was too much, she kept telling him. It wasn't a life she wanted. Sometimes she'd be defiant, determined: it's over, she'd tell him. Then there'd be a day or two's silence and he'd turn up again, all promises and apologies and huge bouquets of flowers like she'd never seen. Then, under the intensity of his persuasion, she'd relent.

In the meantime, suspicious Reg started spying on Frances, sitting in his car, watching her house. He was terrified Frances might go off with another man who tried to get near her.

In May 1964, Pete Whelan, a then 21-year-old printer's apprentice from Clerkenwell, met Frances, then 20, at a Hackney Wimpy bar.

He fell for her beauty and asked her out, sparking a fun three-month relationship, which included romantic trips to the theatre or pubs.

Pete couldn't believe his luck - that this bright, bubbly, arty girl wanted to go on dates with him

He told **The Daily Express**: 'One night I took her to a big family party in South London. My cousin said she looked just like Brigitte Bardot. It was true. Everyone who saw her was saying "Who's that girl"?'

Pete also told how he was made equally welcome by Frances' parents Elsie and Frank whenever he picked her up for a date - both of whom were disapproving of Frances's marriage to Reggie.

But, looking back on the period years later, Pete knew there was an obstacle between him and Frances.

According to Pete, Frances mentioned to him that she had problems - but he had no idea whatsoever that she was being stalked at all times by Reggie Kray's henchmen.

Sometimes, when he dropped Frances off at her house, he would notice an MG Midget patrolling the street, driving past the parked van, but he thought nothing of it.

He added: 'The first time it happened she sat up and tried to see the car. The next time she just slid down in the seat. She seemed a bit troubled but not enough for me to worry about.'

Pete recalled how Frances even once showed him a photo of Reggie, asking if he knew who he was. Pete didn't recognise the notorious gangster.

Then in July, when they'd arranged to go to the theatre one night, Frances's mother came to the door and sent Pete away, saying her daughter was not there. He left and did not speak to Frances again.

Reggie by now had been sent again to prison, this time Brixton. When he was released, he and Frances continued talking about marriage. Unknown to Frances, Reggie had already booked the church, St James the Great in Bethnal Green. He very much wanted the twins' childhood friend and supporter, Father Hetherington, to marry them.

Not merely was there not the faintest hope of either of them finding happiness together, but I could see them causing serious harm to one another

Father Hetherington

But Father Hetherington said he would not be prepared to marry them. 'Because they'd simply no idea of what marriage was about,' the priest said. 'Not merely was there not the faintest hope of either of them finding happiness together, but I could see them causing serious harm to one another.'

Frances was already apprehensive, but she couldn't have known just how accurate Father Hetherington's prediction was.

The day of the wedding was 19 April 1965, an overcast and chilly day. Half a century on, we can look at some of the wedding photos and judge for ourselves how happy they truly seemed.

The photos were taken by the world's most famous photographer, David Bailey, an East End boy whose fame was already soaring sky high in the sixties. Many other celebrities were on the guest list. But the atmosphere? Heavy as lead.

For their honeymoon, the couple stayed in an Athens hotel. Reg went out drinking most night, often leaving his bride alone in their hotel. A series of diary entries in Frances's own handwriting chronicle some detail of their troubled marriage.

Soon, Frances was no longer the starry-eyed young girl. She was Reggie's missus, his property. Socially, she'd clammed up. 'She was in a situation she couldn't handle,' recalled Freddie Foreman, the 'Godfather of crime' who served ten years in prison for his role in the disposal of the boy of Jack 'The Hat' McVitie, and who met Frances many times in the clubland setting.

'She used to sit there like a pretty little thing. She did not talk or converse with anyone, it was a different world to what she was used to.'

The rows between them became hideously abusive. One night, knowing she hated the sight of blood, Reggie deliberately cut his hand and tormented her by letting the blood drip onto her. It was terrifying emotional abuse for an already nervous and edgy girl. There were also allegations that Reggie had sex with a prostitute while Frances lay asleep next to them. The shocking incident could have been the trigger that made Frances pack her bags and return to her family that summer. Once safely back with her family, Frances recounted some of what had been going on. She said she felt ashamed, soiled, degraded. No other man would want her now.

But Reg could not bring himself to stay away. Or allow Frances to have her own life. As traumatic as those weeks after the marriage had been for her, the suffering woman - who was by now dependent on sleeping tablets - was still unable to disassociate herself with Reggie completely. The truth is, he would not let her out of his life. If she did attempt to 'escape' there was always the threat - which Frances believed - that the Kray network could seek anyone out, no matter where they went. Let alone what they could do to their family.

So despite all the turmoil that had gone down between them, they would up in this strange place of emotional dependency, neither together nor quite apart.

One night I took her to a big family party in South London. My cousin said she looked just like Brigitte Bardot. It was true. Everyone who saw her was saying "Who's that girl"?

Pete Whelan

That summer, Frances received shock treatment, commonly used to treat depression then. She was still trapped in the Kray web, shunned by many out of ignorance or fear. Whatever Frances was hearing or being told about Reggie via the local whispers would only have served to exacerbate her fears, her terror. She was embarking on a perilous road towards self-destruction.

At the time, Frances was buying street drugs. She was then admitted to hospital, as a result of an overdose of barbiturates. More suicide attempts followed.

In the summer of 1967, Reggie and Frances were reunited. But while Frances seemed outwardly to accept having Reggie back in her life, one might pause to question her motivation

Did she just go along with it to keep the peace? Reggie's motivation was surely partly driven by what was happening to him and Ronnie, as the net of the law started to close in on them. In all probability, Frances was too diminished by everything she'd experienced to push him away or make big demands. She was exhausted. It was easier to just pretend.

Reg suggested a second honeymoon at the end of June in Ibiza. Yes, she said, they could do that. On 5 June, Frances went for an appointment at Hackney Hospital and seemed a bit brighter. The following day, she saw Reg and they booked the tickets at a local travel agent. They farewelled each other and her brother's flat and Reg went home.

But, two days later, her brother Frankie found her. That morning of June 7, he took his sister a cup of tea, as he usually did, carefully placing it on the bedside table. She seemed to be still sleeping peacefully, so he went out to work. Yet something, he couldn't quite explain what, sent him back to check on his sister around lunchtime. She was just as he'd left her earlier. The tea was stone cold. Maybe it was an accident, and she took one pill too many? She couldn't have planned it, many argued. They were looking forward to going away, weren't they? These were false hopes. Frances had been merely biding her time, pretending to Reg about the holding, knowing full well she'd never be going anywhere with him again.

Frances's funeral was as ostentatious as Reggie wished. At the time, the story went round that the funeral cost ran to £2,000 - the equivalent of around £30,000 today. Reggie ordered huge floral wreaths, one in a heart shape with red roses and white carnations going through the middle, the biggest one being a six-foot tall wreath spelling out her name.

Yet, with a few months, as the Shea family struggled with their loss, the grief-stricken husband would be finding comfort in the arms of a 23-year-old woman. And a man answering to the name of McVitie would be meeting a grisly end.

Once inside, the duo capitalised on their criminal and celebrity status, ensuring that their stay in Her Majesty's prison system was truly, and historically, unique.

Maureen Flanagan, a tabloid model and actress, knew the Krays well - and acted as the twins' liaison with the outside world after their imprisonment. "As the boys were Category A prisoners," Flanagan explains, "only family were allowed to visit them to begin with. So their mother, Violet, would come back from visits with a big long list of things they wanted and I had to go out and find. They were quite greedy, considering they were in jail!"

The brothers were soon separated when Ronnie was diagnosed as a paranoid schizophrenic and moved to Broadmoor Hospital, a high-security psychiatric facility. Ronnie began to settle once he was moved out of the standard prison system, where he had been misunderstood, attacked by prison officers and goaded into fighting other inmates.

"I used to take a tailor into Broadmoor twice a year to sort Ron out. Can you imagine that? And I used to take him a selection of Giorgio Armani or Hugo Boss ties. When I used to visit, all the other people were sitting there in old, coffee-stained jumpers and trousers and then Ronnie Kray used to come out immaculately dressed, looking like a Harley Street doctor.

"When he needed new glasses he told me: 'I don't want any of this National Health Service nonsense, I want nice tortoiseshell frames'. Even people in fashion used to send him shirts! But he only ever kept half of them, gave the other half away to the other prisoners. I think he was trying to smarten up the jail!"

The Kray twins, although characterised by the unforgivably violent outbursts that landed them in jail, undoubtedly had a more compassionate side. The twins gave generously to charity, and the rehabilitating effects of prison seemed to amplify this altruism.

"There was this one time when Ronnie told me that he wanted me to get him a guitar," recounts Flanagan. "He told me to go down to Tin Pan Alley, 'where Eric Clapton buys his guitars', and buy one for him. And this was all because he wanted to give it to a lad he knew inside for a Christmas present.

"Once Ronnie moved to Broadmoor," Flanagan recalls, "he was much happier. You could decorate your own room and, as you can imagine, Ronnie's room was absolutely spotless. That was the thing about Ronnie – he had this cross-personality where he would go out and commit these acts of violence, but he'd never want to even drive a car out of fear that it would dirty his hands.

"He chain-smoked about 80 cigarettes a day, but never took more than two or three puffs on each one – and that was for the same reason. He didn't want tobacco-stained fingers. And it worked. I never once saw a stain on Ronnie Kray's hands." Reggie endured a considerably tougher prison experience. Ronnie's twin was transferred between six geographically-diverse prisons in quick succession - a move his friends and family believed to be part of the judicial system's ploy to break his spirit. Missing Ronnie, Reggie became dangerously depressed and began having visions and hearing voices - troubling episodes that culminated in him smashing the glass window of his wristwatch and slashing his wrists with the shards.

Maureen Flanagan remembers the incident, but believes that after reaching the bottom of his mental descent, Reggie began to mentally rebuild and acclimatise to life inside. Ronnie, by comparison, was living easy inside Broadmoor, free to indulge his hobbies and sending Flanagan off around London to search for various obscure luxuries and goods.

"Every month I had to take Ronnie certain things. Smoked salmon and cream cheese bagels, he loved them. And pork pies. But the pork pies had to come from Harrods and the bagels from Brick Lane. He went through a box of 100 Player's cigarettes every single day, but gave quite a few of them away inside. He was really quite a generous man, Ronnie.

"He loved his records, too. Opera though. I remember he once had me running about looking for a Puccini LP to play on his little gramophone. And particular bed linen, he wanted that. He didn't like the things they were provided with in Broadmoor – he called it 'ordinary stuff'."

As Ronnie Kray was confined in Broadmoor - where detainees are referred to as 'patients' rather than 'inmates' - he was not required to wear a standard issue prison uniform. This meant that the twin could once meet the sartorial standards of his street attire, even though he was behind bars.

"He gave me the money, I went and bought one and asked the man in the shop if they did deliveries. 'Yes', he says, 'where to?' and I say, 'Ronnie Kray, Broadmoor'. And he just looked at me. I asked him if he was sure it'd get there before Christmas and he just looked at me some more and said 'it's Ronnie Kray, would we dare not deliver the thing on time?'"

It would be these instances of morality-blurring behaviour that would typify Ronnie and Reggie's time inside. Despite being motivated by seemingly worthy intentions, the twins still were not above using their reputations of intimidation and threat to get what they wanted.

David Fraser, an ex-con and son of gangland enforcer "Mad" Frankie Fraser, spent time with Reggie Kray whilst the two were imprisoned together in HM Prison Lewes. "I hadn't seen him for years," remembers Fraser, "but he came down the morning I was put in, just to say hello. He used to have all these lads in his room - 'stargazers' he called them. He liked their attention, telling them stories and stuff. He was very friendly, always on hand to give some advice. Straight people find this very hard to believe, but Reggie Kray was actually a really nice man."

"He was always on the phone, mind. And then one day I desperately needed to make a call - my mum wasn't well. I asked Reg and he got straight off the phone, then asked me how she was after I hung up. And he really wanted to know too. I rang my mum back up once she'd got better and she said to me, 'it was really nice of that Reggie Kray, sending me such a big bouquet of flowers'. And I never knew he had until she said that, he hadn't told me."

The twins' acts of quiet giving were construed as repentance by all that knew the Krays. Maureen Flanagan remembers how whilst Ronnie liked to amass luxuries and extravagant gifts to show his affection for people, all Reggie ever asked for inside was writing paper, stamps and envelopes.

"I was speaking to some people at the premiere [of Legend] last week," Flanagan shares, "and some of the people there had just written to Reggie back when he was in jail - without any hope of a reply. But they always got one. If you wrote to Reggie, you got an answer, no matter who you were – he wrote around 20 letters every day."

"And people who wrote to Reg used to ask him for money or help, for their children who might have had multiple sclerosis, or cancer or something like that, and he'd really want to help. So he'd have me running all over London setting up fundraising events and charity auctions at pubs."

Flanagan's stories of Reggie Kray's benevolence tally with David Fraser's tales of the twin, whom he remembers as a charitable man. "His name cropped up in so many books around then, did Reggie. And that film with the Kemp brothers. He told me that him and his brothers got £85,000 each for that picture. But when I asked him what he was going to do with the cash, he said he'd donated it all already."

The Krays were rumoured to be keeping up appearances whilst behind bars, constantly planning for that elusive day on which they would be released. And from the openly homosexual Ronnie marrying Elaine Mildener to the twins taking up oil painting to illustrate their expectations of freedom, the evidence suggested that the two truly believed that they would eventually have a life beyond prison walls.
But the money tells a different story and, despite allegedly amassing more capital inside than they ever did on the out, David Fraser believes the twins were charitable with their cash because they secretly knew that they would die behind bars. "I think," muses Fraser, "deep down inside, they both knew they were never going to get out."

and, at the ages of 61 and 66 respectively, Ronnie and Reggie Kray indeed died whilst still serving their sentences.

The twins' time in prison was markedly different to their lives on the outside, and from Ronnie's comfortable, designer days to the varied and often suicidally difficult prison career of Reggie, their crime spree on the streets of London was undoubtedly only half of their story.

But did these years of imprisonment lead to repentance? Fraser believes so. "I was once walking around the exercise yard with Reggie, talking about what he done, and he turned to me and just said: "It was just so silly. All of it. Though it always is afterwards, isn't it?"

The cost of living then 1960s : 20p a pint, and a Mini for £600

With the benefit of 47 years' hindsight, life in 1969 appears to have been ludicrously cheap. A loaf of bread cost 9p and the average weekly wage was around £32. Today, a loaf costs 53p and weekly wages are about £475. Property prices have also risen. In 1970, homebuyers could expect to pay £4,975 for a house. Today, their children would not get much change from £140,000.

It was a similar story on the roads. The Range Rover, which was launched in 1970, could have been yours for £1,998. Almost a quarter of a century later, a 4.4 litre Range Rover Vogue will set you back £57,700.

The Mini, which celebrated its 11th birthday in 1970, cost around £600. Its redesigned descendant now sells for £10,500.

HOW PRICES HAVE CHANGED IN 49 YEARS

	1960	2009	Change %			1960	2009	Change %
loaf	4.5p	£1.26	2,764		Barbie doll	£1.70	£17	900
r (llb)	22p	£2.10	854		Eggs (half a dozen, medium)	16p	£2.66	1,605
l pint)	3.3p	45p	1,264		FA Cup Final ticket	£2.50	From £35	1,300
	£496	£12,345	2,389		Fish and chips	6p	£4.50	7,400
(1 kg)	6.5p	88p	1,254		Potatoes (1 kg)	3p	69p	2,200
50g)	16.5p	£1.81	977		20 cigarettes	20p	£5.39	2,595
s (lkg)	11p	£1.51	1,272					
l (ltr)	5p	86p	1,620					

Source: National Statistics (1960 figures converted to modern £/p)

A glance at Britain's social life in 1970 is equally intriguing. A trip for two to the cinema cost less than 90p, compared with at least £9 today, while a bottle of plonk was about £1. Today it is £4.55.

 For those with more spirited and extravagant tastes, a bottle of whisky cost £2.69 back then, compared with £12 now. Pub prices, too, seem foreign. A pint of lager in your local was 20p, a far cry from today's average of £2.10. And cigarettes, which enjoyed a lot more popularity then, were 20p for 20. Today, the habit costs about £4.65 a pack.
Still, it's not all doom and gloom. Prices have gone up but so has our spending power.
And some things have even risen for the better. In 1969, the average life expectancy in Britain was 72. Today, it is 77 - giving us five more years of spending.

Kray sups champagne at hotel on first night of freedom

Reggie Kray, who was released from prison on compassionate grounds, was toasting his freedom last night with champagne.

Reggie Kray, who was released from prison on compassionate grounds, was toasting his freedom last night with champagne.

The former gangland boss, 66, who has inoperable bowel cancer, left the Norfolk and Norwich Hospital yesterday and is staying at a £37.50-a-night Beefeater hotel on the outskirts of Norwich with his wife, Roberta, 41, and their security men.

He also felt well enough for two sandwiches and a glass of whisky at lunchtime before moving on to champagne. John Brunton, a publican and friend of the Krays, said he had been keen to have a room with a view of the river Wensum. "As soon as he arrived in the room we drew back the curtains so that he could enjoy the view.

"Water is something he has been desperate to see, simply because he hasn't seen it for 32 years. We chose this hotel because it was the nearest place we could find with a river view. He is delighted with the way he has settled in," Mr Brunton said.

Kray was given a life sentence at the Old Bailey in 1969 after being convicted of stabbing Jack "The Hat" McVitie to death in a flat in Stoke Newington, north London. He was freed on 26 August this year by Jack Straw, the Home Secretary, because of deteriorating health. It was said that he had already planned his funeral.

He was moved to hospital from Wayland prison, near Watton, Norfolk, 10 days earlier and was widely expected to die there, but his solicitor, Mark Goldstein, said his condition had stabilised and he was able to leave. He had been overwhelmed by the number of cards and telephone calls wishing him well, Mr Goldstein added. "He would like everyone to know that the continuing support provides the strength to battle against the cancer." Mr Brunton said: "We are hoping that, without any pressure, this will give him longer to live... a matter of months rather than weeks. This is freedom for him."

"Kray chose the Town House because he wanted to look out over a river "

East End says farewell to last of the Krays

THE amplified tones of Frank Sinatra rolled across an East End churchyard as the coffin of Reginald Kray, Sixties gangland leader and convicted murderer, was carried from church by six pallbearers.

Reginald Kray's coffin is carried from St Matthew's Church, Bethnal Green

Kray had asked that My Way should be the final song played at his funeral service yesterday. "Regrets, I've had a few," crooned Sinatra's voice. "But then again, too few to mention." Mourners at St Matthew's Church, Bethnal Green, were told that Kray's regrets for his violent criminal past were not a subject anyone wanted to dwell on.

This was a day for lionising Kray, who **died from cancer on Oct 1**, just over a month after being **released from prison on compassionate grounds** having served 32 years for murder. Mark Goldstein, Kray's solicitor, told the congregation that the man they had come to remember was "an icon of the 20th century" who possessed "an amazing sense of humour".

More than that, said Ken Stallard, delivering the funeral address, Kray had been a man in search of God. Mr Stallard, an Evangelical Free Church minister, described himself as Kray's spiritual adviser for the past 17 years, having met the killer through his twin brother Ronald, also a convicted murderer.

Dr Stallard said: "In both of these men were depths of spiritual feeling which the world never saw nor knew. So many people preferred to look at the bad rather than the good. Reg spent a great deal of money and a great deal of time looking after and caring for others."

Mr Stallard said that Kray repented for his crimes and became a convert to Christianity. But the minister had been told to keep the conversion secret in case people thought it a ruse to seek release on parole. Dr Stallard's words were relayed by loudspeaker to hundreds of people who braved a bitter wind to listen to the service in the churchyard.

Many had walked from the funeral parlour of W English & Son on Bethnal Green Road following the hearse, drawn by six black stallions adorned with feathered head plumes and wearing shining patent leather and silver harness, which bore Kray's coffin.

TOM HARDY plays both Ronnie and Reggie in the film — and watching him in action on screen was like seeing the twins reincarnated.
His physical likeness to both is uncanny. It was like watching their ghosts looming from 50 years ago. But one thing the film gets totally wrong is the relationship between Reggie and his wife, Frances Shea. It portrays him to be a Romeo who charms all the birds off the trees, and that could not be more wrong.

He was gay, just like Ronnie.

The film gives the impression that Frances killed herself because she couldn't cope with Reggie being a gangster or being drawn into violence by his brother, and all that cobblers.

The truth is that their marriage was never properly consummated and she referred to him as "bacon bonce", which is Cockney rhyming slang for nonce.

The film also gives the impression that Reggie was a fun-loving, cheeky chap who fancied himself as a businessman but got dragged down by his nutty brother.

It wasn't like that at all.

Reg shot and stabbed people for next to nothing. He took liberties. Once he went to the home of one guy on the Firm at 7.30am and shot him in front of his wife and kids. That was just for taking Ronnie's side in an argument.

And the film makes Ronnie out to be a psychopathic lunatic, but actually he was a very warm person and capable of great kindness. He also had a very good sense of humour.

Yes, he did walk into the Blind Beggar pub and shoot George Cornell dead. But in the earlier days, Ron was still not as bad as the film makes out.

There was an aura of fear about both twins and the film gets that across well. If they were around, everybody was on their best behaviour.

But they were also polite and never swore in front of women or raised their voices in public. I'm not sure the film gets that across.

1. 178 Vallance Road

Though born in Stean Street, Hoxton, the twins soon moved to this address in Bethnal Green. The actual house no longer exists, but to see the childhood home from the movie, head to Canrobert Street, on the other side of the Bethnal Green Road, where filming took place. Teesdale Street, which runs parallel to Canrobert, also features.

2. The Blind Beggar

One of the best known Kray locations, this Whitechapel pub is where Ronnie shot and killed George Cornell. It is still a thriving venue, now serving up posh hot dogs and boasting a smart beer garden with a fancy water feature – we're not sure what the twins would make of that…

3. Pellicci's Café

This celebrated greasy spoon on the Bethnal Green Road was a favoured haunt of the Krays. It also appears in the new Tom Hardy film.

178 Vallance Road now
and in 1960s

Pellicci's Café

The Blind Beggar

4. Esmeralda's Barn

This Knightsbridge nightclub was owned by the Krays from 1960 until its closure in 1963. They turned it into a gambling club, whose regulars included Francis Bacon and Lucien Freud. The site is now home to The Berkeley, a five-star hotel.

5. Bow Street Magistrates' Court

The Krays were among numerous famous defendants to appear at Bow Street during its 266-year existence (others include Oscar Wilde, Emmeline Pankhurst, General Pinochet and Giocomo Casanova). It closed in 2006 and has long been tipped for redevelopment as a boutique hotel.

6. Tower of London

In 1952, the twins were among the last prisoners to be held at the Tower of London after they failed to report for national service, joining a long list of notable figures that includes Rudolf Hess, Sir Robert Walpole, Samuel Pepys and Guy Fawkes.

Ron and Reg with the stars

their first toehold in this area was an upmarket gaming club called Esmeraldas. It was fronted by Lord Effingham, the sixth Earl of Effingham

Lord Boothby, Ronnie Kray and Leslie Holt

kray twins murder victims george cornell and jack
the hat mcvitie

Frank Mitchell (the 'Mad Axeman')

Ron and Reg

Reg Kray Deathbed murder confession

Other Murders
Mad Teddy Smith never seen again

Never seen since 1967

Also The Metropolitan Police are to investigate

The Metropolitan Police are to investigate claims that Ronnie Kray killed his brother's wife.
An inquest at the time concluded Frances Kray had committed suicide.
Reggie Kray's gay lover has claimed that Frances was forced by Ronnie to take the pills that killed her.
However Reggie's widow, Roberta Kray, said Bradley Allardyce had misunderstood her late husband, who had not meant it literally.
Mrs Kray said: "Reg told me on several occasions that Ron had killed Frances but he didn't mean it in a literal sense. 190

Kray family graves are vandalised

VANDALS sprayed obscene graffiti on the gravestones of notorious gangsters Ronnie and Reggie Kray and their mother, Violet.

Their brother Charlie and Reggie's wife Francis's gravestones were also vandalised on February 23.

A council spokesman said: "Headstones on the Kray family plot in Chingford were graffitied with black spray paint. This incident occurred some time during the day and the paint was cleaned off as soon as staff were notified of the problem."

He said the nature of the graffiti could not be revealed.

The Kray twins inspired fear throughout the London underworld in the 1960s and achieved notoriety when they were jailed for the killing of two other gangsters in 1969.

A local man who saw the graves said: "It was disgusting. That sort of thing shouldn't happen, no matter who you are."

A few drawings from Reg Kray

Reg kray drawing while in jail

"Stay Strong"

1994

Art work of the krays

Ron Kray

Painting by ron kray while at Broadmoor

Public 'never told' about Broadmoor hospital riot

Police and NHS officials failed to make public a riot at Broadmoor hospital, where scores of Britain's most dangerous criminals are held, Freedom of Information disclosures reveal.

Ambulance crews and police officers in riot gear were called to Britain's most high-profile secure unit after violence flared on a ward which houses patients with dangerous personality disorders.

During the incident, patients took over the nurses' office, and are alleged to have obtained medical notes of other residents of the hospital, which is home to some of Britain's most notorious criminals.

Although the incident occurred last July, police and hospital officials failed to make the matter public.

Three months before the incident, regulators were alerted to concerns about "inadequate levels of staffing" on the ward, and concern that too many hospital patients were being put in seclusion.

A spokeswoman for West London Mental Health trust, which runs Broadmoor, denied that the riot was linked to staff shortages

. She refused to confirm or deny reports that during the incident, patients gained access to others' medical notes, and that some had to be transferred elsewhere because of what had been accessed.

The trust said the incident did not amount to a riot, and involved two patients who broke into a ward office, with emergency staff called in as back up.

The trust said the ward sustained damage during the incident. However the spokeswoman refused to provide details about the costs of repairs on the grounds this would indicate "the nature and scale" of what had occurred.

The trust said it had fully investigated the incident but refused to release its report on the matter, stating that doing so could compromise hospital security.

The incident occurred on a 12 bed ward, Epsom Ward, which houses patients with complex and challenging personality disorders, some of whom can be dangerous.

In 2010 a nurse on the same ward was given a suspended sentence after having a sexual relationship with a convicted rapist and arsonist.

The hospital houses Peter Sutcliffe – the Yorkshire Ripper – who was jailed for the murder of 13 women and the attempted murder of others in Yorkshire and Greater Manchester in the 1970s.

South Central Ambulance Service trust said two people were treated by its crews at the scene of the incident and that it sent a "hazardous area response team" to the hospital.

Thames Valley Police said they sent a "public order response" - meaning police officers in riot gear - but that the incident was resolved using hospital staff.

Broadmoor Hospital

Peter William Sutcliffe is an English serial killer who was dubbed The Yorkshire Ripper. Sutcliffe was convicted in 1981 of murdering 13 women and attacking several others. He is currently serving life imprisonment in Broadmoor. Reportedly a loner at school, he left at the age of 15 and took a series of menial jobs, including two stints as a grave digger during the 1960s. He frequented prostitutes as a young man and it has been speculated that a bad experience with one (during which he was allegedly conned out of money) helped fuel his violent hatred against women.

In 1981, Sutcliffe was stopped by the police with a 24 year old prostitute. A police check revealed the car was fitted with false number plates and Sutcliffe was arrested for this offence and transferred to Dewsbury Police Station, West Yorkshire. At Dewsbury he was questioned in relation to the Yorkshire Ripper case as he matched so many of the physical characteristics known. The next day police returned to the scene of the arrest and discovered a knife, hammer and rope he discarded when he briefly slipped away from police during the arrest. After two days of intensive questioning, on the afternoon of 4 January 1981 Sutcliffe suddenly declared he was the Ripper. Over the next day, Sutcliffe calmly described his many attacks. Weeks later he claimed God told him to murder the women. He displayed emotion only when telling of the murder of his youngest victim, Jayne MacDonald.

At his trial, Sutcliffe pleaded not guilty to 13 counts of murder, but guilty to manslaughter on the grounds of diminished responsibility. The basis of this defence was his claim that he was the tool of God's will. Sutcliffe first claimed to have heard voices while working as a gravedigger, that ultimately ordered him to kill prostitutes. He claimed that the voices originated from a headstone of a deceased Polish man, Bronislaw Zapolski, and that the voices were that of God.

In the years of Sutcliffe's incarceration, there have been numerous attempts on his life from other inmates. The first was during his stay at HMP Parkhurst when James Costello, a 35-year-old career criminal from Glasgow plunged a broken coffee jar twice into the left side of Sutcliffe's face. Whilst at Broadmoor he was subject to an attempted strangulation (thwarted by Kenneth Erskine, above) and lost the vision in his left eye after being attacked with a pen.

Peter William
Sutcliffe

Charles "Charlie" Bronson (born Michael Gordon Peterson) is an English criminal often referred to in the British press as the "most violent prisoner in Britain". Born in Luton, England, Michael often found his way into fights before he began a bare-knuckle boxing career in the East End of London. His promoter was not happy with his name and suggested he change it to Charles Bronson.

In 1974 he was imprisoned for a robbery and sentenced to seven years. While in prison he began making a name for himself as a loose cannon often fighting convicts and prison guards. These fights added years onto his sentence. Regarded as a problem prisoner, he was moved 120 times throughout Her Majesty's Prison Service and spent all but 4 years of his imprisoned life in solitary confinement. What was originally a seven year term stretched out to fourteen year sentence that resulted in his first wife Irene, with whom he had a son, leaving him. He was released on October 30, 1988 but only spent 69 days free before he was arrested again. Bronson has spent a total of just four months and nine days out of custody since 1974. Known as one of the hardest criminals in England, Bronson has written many books about his experiences and famous prisoners he has met throughout his internment.

Bronson has been involved in over a dozen hostage incidents, one of which includes taking hostages and staging a 47-hour rooftop protest at Broadmoor in 1983, causing £750,000 (nearly $1.5m) worth of damage. Bronson has spent time at all three of England's high-security psychiatric hospitals.

Charles "Charlie" Bronson (born Michael Gordon Peterson)

David John Copeland is a former member of the British National Party and the National Socialist Movement, who became known as the "London Nail Bomber," after a 13-day bombing campaign in April 1999 aimed at London's black, Bangladeshi and gay communities. The bombs killed three, including a pregnant woman, and injured 129, four of whom lost limbs. No warnings were given.

After his arrest, he told psychiatrists that he had started having sadistic dreams when he was about 12, including dreams or fantasies that he had been reincarnated as an SS officer with access to women as slaves. Copeland wrote to BBC correspondent Graeme McLagan, denying that he had schizophrenia, and telling McLagan that the "ZOG," or Zionist Occupation Government, was pumping him full of drugs in order to sweep him under the carpet. He wrote, "I bomb the blacks, Pakis, degenerates. I would have bombed the Jews as well if I'd got a chance". When asked by police why he had targeted ethnic minorities, he replied: "Because I don't like them, I want them out of this country, I believe in the master race.

Although Copeland was diagnosed by five psychiatrists as having paranoid schizophrenia, and a consultant concluded he had a personality disorder, his plea of diminished responsibility was not accepted by the prosecution, which was under pressure not to concede to his pleas of guilty to manslaughter. He was convicted of murder on June 30, 2000, and given six concurrent life sentences.

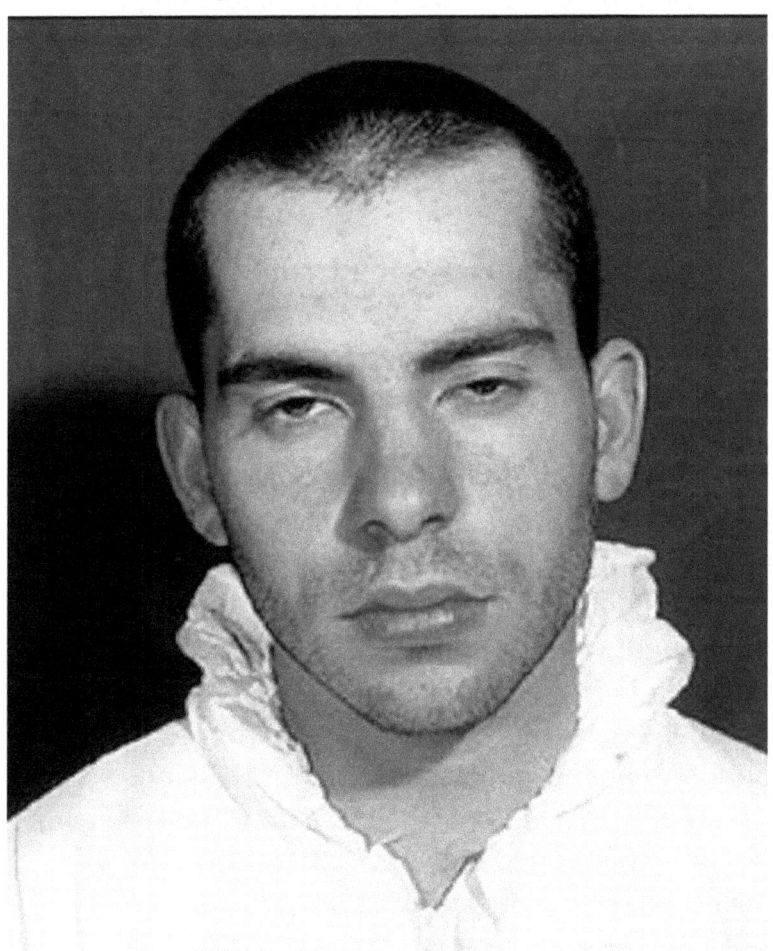

David John Copeland is a former member of the British National Party

tape recording made by Frances Kray, on a Walter reel-to-reel tape recorder at her family home, with the voices of her parents, intervals of music and herself, first mimicking a Sarsens Vinegar advertisement in a mock `upper class` accent, then saying; `...just going to mess about with this damned machine...if you don`t mind...I know Bacon Bonce would mind, but he`s not here...probably up his stinking club...`

Note: `Bacon Bonce` - cockney rhyming slang for `nonce`, i.e. child molester (apparently referring to Reggie Kray]

An interesting autograph letter from Reggie Kray to Frances Shea (Sunday 1st December 1963), written from the Catering Rest House, Enugu, Nigeria, it describes the hotel and its desolate surroundings, `snobbish types` and `good humoured` Nigerians that he meets and mentions `business` talks with `Ron` (also referring to `Les`), how much he misses her, etc

Note: Ronald Kray was involved with Ernest Shinwell in trying to finance a deal to help build a new town near Enugu. Whilst Ronnie enjoyed three days of VIP treatment in Nigeria, Leslie Payne, the Krays business manager was setting up holding companies in London to act as vehicles for the fund-raising. Presumably this letter relates to a later trip to Nigeria. The `Les` mentioned may be East End cat burglar, Leslie Holt, who along with his illicit lover, Lord Boothby, was also involved in the project, which eventually collapsed.

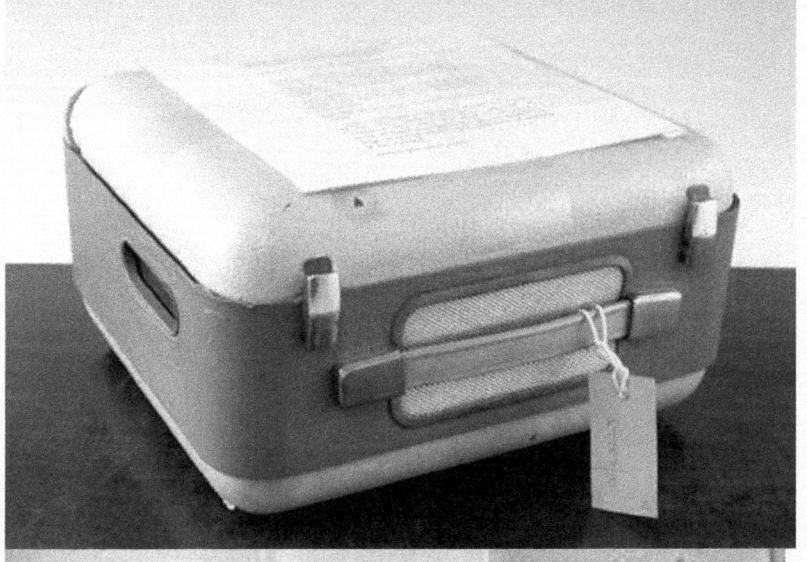

Death with a View

You turn to your dinner companion with a smile that suddenly freezes on your face when the glass you were about to drink from is thrown from the table by an invisible hand.

You stay the night and someone or something opens your bedroom door. You go to the washroom and the hairs on the back of your neck stand up as you feel the presence that no one can explain. Oh - and the other thing about this hotel……the reported ghost of a feared and iconic figure from 1960s London who died in room 4. Disrespect is not an option.

Twice we have held public paranormal investigations at this picturesque riverside hotel in Norwich, situated on a side water of the river Wensum and overlooking a small island. With superb views over the South West edge of the Norfolk broads it's difficult to imagine that death (and a famous death at that) could mar this idyllic setting. There have been other deaths in the past, just as famous in their day but not in our era. The site dates back to 1720 and was once a row of cottages which were later combined into one. It has been a hotel since 1930 but prior to that in 1841 it was owned by Edmund Cotman.

It is believed that he bought the house in an attempt to provide some relief to his ailing son John Sell Cotman (1782-1842) a famous son of Norwich and a member of the Norwich School of Painters. The view from the hotel formed the basis of his last painting (From my Father's House at Thorpe. 1842)

Our recent investigation uncovered a number of anomalies, from temperature fluctuations of up to 25 degrees F in room 4 where we used the Planchette, to unaccountable EMF meter readings and contact with a number of Spirits in room 19 and the corridors. Three separate groups picked up a young girl called Sarah with blonde hair who drowned in the river.

The Table Tipping in the bar area was a bit hit and miss, some groups got nothing at all and others had lots of movement, in particular when the name of the person who died in room 4 was mentioned.

The Glass moving on table 15 was more active, maybe because of the energy that has been known to move the drinking glasses of unsuspecting diners; however when the special name was mentioned the glass almost flew off the table and had to be caught to prevent it smashing onto the floor.

Coincidence? We don't know for sure.

All we do know is we had to be very careful not to be disrespectful of any of the resident Spirits just in case one of them was the man who, not too long ago, died in room 4.

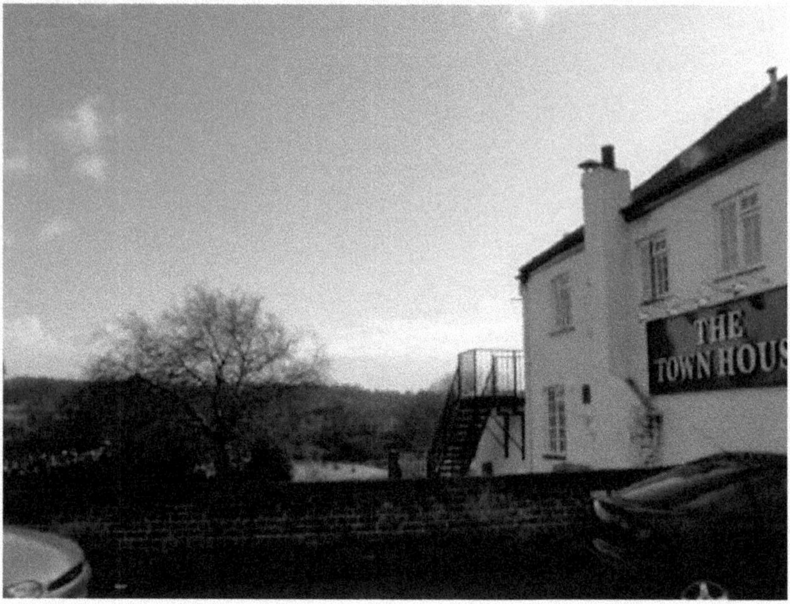
THE
TOWN HOUS

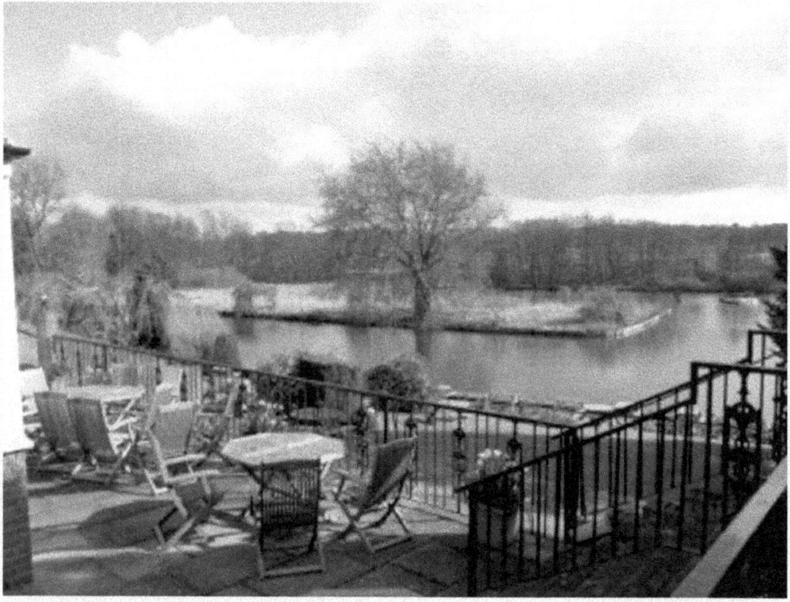

THE TOWN HOUSE

18-22 Yarmouth Road, Thorpe St Andrew,
Norwich,Norfolk, NR7 0EF

Call us:**01603 700600**

Reg Kray last home

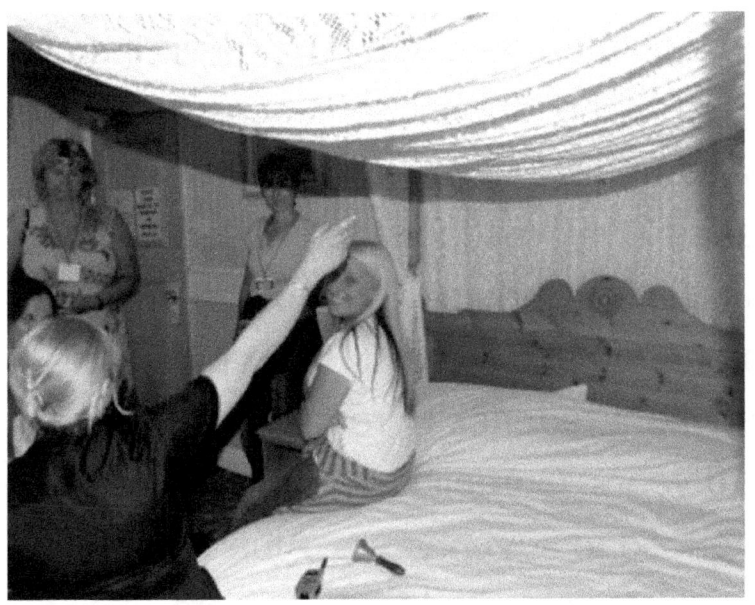

The Firm above

The Kray twins were both sentenced to life imprisonment with a recommendation they should be detained for a minimum of 30 years - the longest sentences ever passed at the Old Bailey for murder. Charles Kray was jailed for 10 years. John Barrie, Christopher and Anthony Lambrianou and Ronald Bender were all given life. Frederick Foreman was jailed for 10 years. Cornelius Whitehead was sentenced to seven years. Albert Donaghue was jailed for two years.

BROTHERHOOD
OF
EVIL

Sentence today on the Krays after 'guilty' verdict

By
HARRY LONGMUIR and
ARTHUR TIETJEN

Brotherly handclasp of friendship : Reginald Kray, left, and twin Ronald, right, guilty of murder. Charles, centre, sentence to...

TWINS Ronald and Reginald Kray and four members of their 'firm' were found guilty last night of murder.

Three others, including eldest Kray brother Charles, were convicted as accessories after murder.

All this, and a much man who admitted being an accessory, will be detained at the Old Bailey today by Mr Justice Melford Stevenson.

Anthony Thomas Barry, 37, night club partner, who was cleared by the judge after the jury had failed to agree in the case of murder, was the only one acquitted of any part and was discharged.

Mr Charles Kray, senior, father of the three brothers, who watched the entire 39-day trial, told us he felt the acquittal of his youngest son was a devine bubble.

The photograph on the right is Ronald.

One by one

The toll for the four-storm examination came at 7 p.m. after the jury of 12 men had been out for almost seven hours.

Then decided unanimously that Ronald Kray had murdered twice and finished of kills. Reginald Kray was found guilty of the murder of Jack McVitie.

Only for eighty-hude Anthony Barry did the verdict ... change — Guilty ... for the member of the firm, who cleared on the Krays by ...

As he left the dock Barry, of The Burning Road, Barkingside, Ilford, was greeted by his wife, June, and his three brothers Michael, John and Cecil. They went off to a champagne party to their parents' for breakfast.

Late last night the nine police men were driven by the fast blue in the great security measures from ... Bristol and Wandsworth prisons to be kept ...

Ronald Kray greeted his brother in the interrogation. The judge refused the bars to discharged one and telling them all the ...

He said their 'The

Customs seize the Shah's guns

THREE of the Shah of Persia's bodyguards had a number of machine-guns seized by Customs men at Heathrow Airport, London, last night.

The bodyguards, who guided from Tehran, were told that the guns were unlawful weapons under Section 5 of the Firearms Act ...

All the arms will be handed back to-day, when the bodyguards fly on to Zurich, in Switzerland, where the Shah is ...

The bodyguards spent the night in London.

'Lady C morals' cost students £1

Student behaviour at Town University means Lady Chatterley's Lover like a vicarage teaparty as convections, clearly prompted Mr George Wilson said yesterday.

Town County Council cleared Mr Wilson's complaint that they spend £250,000 grant for the university, at Colchester, should be cut by ...

Play goes on

A distant star on Glenn music should not to influence its protest! ITV broadcasting the play Soldiers about Sir Winston Churchill, was resumed at the hands yesterday by Lord Stockleton, leader of the Peers.

Wall Street

NEW YORK.—Prices went ahead on Wall Street stock market and the Dow Jones industrial index closed 13.19 up at 929.35. Total volume turnover 1,590,000 shares at 3.30 GMT.

Ideal Home Show opens on Wednesday

THE DAILY MAIL Ideal Home Exhibition ... delayed by industrial troubles, will open in Olympia, London, next Wednesday.

It will continue until Saturday, March 29, as arranged. This means that the public will have ... days this year in which to enjoy the show.

Reprieve for carriers?

By ALAN YOUNG

A HINT of a possible re-prieve for Britain's fleet-smoking aircraft carriers was given in the Commons last night.

Mr John Morris, Minister of Defence for Equipment, said he warned telco all Herbert ...

... was being given increased performance, and the Government was now considering basing it on ...

The carriers—Hermes, Ark Royal and Eagle—are due to be phased out of service since the East of Suez withdrawal.

BOXING! A GREAT NIGHTS BOXING BOXING!
MANOR PLACE BATHS
SOUTH LONDON
GEN. MANAGER LARSH   A FREDDIE FOREMAN PROMOTION   MATCHMAKER JIM DEPT ESO

DOORS OPEN 7.00 p.m. ## SATURDAY 16TH JUNE **BOXING STARTS 8.00 p.m.**

THE EXCITING UP AND COMING KRAY TWINS
RONNIE
KRAY
NON STOP PUNCHING MACHINE **BETHNAL GREEN**
V
AL GUNNING
SOUTH AFRICAN CHAMPION

6 X 3 MINUTE ROUNDS

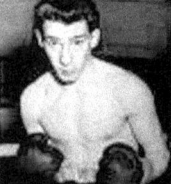

A CHAMPION IN THE MAKING "CLASS" ACT
REGGIE
KRAY
BETHNAL GREEN
V
BILLY AMBROSE
HACKNEY

6 X 3 MINUTE ROUNDS

ARTHUR MALLARD	TERRY DOWNS	6 X 3 ROUNDS WELTERWEIGHT
HOXTON SOUTHERN HEAVYWEIGHT CHAMP	PADDINGTON	HARRY PIKE
6 X 3 ROUNDS	V	EXCITING BOX FIGHTER
V	HARRY STARBUCK	MILE END
JOHNNY WALLSNR	SOUTH LONDON	V
A WONDERFUL PROSPECT	OUTSTANDING PROSPECT	CHARLIE KRAY
LONDON		BETHNAL GREEN

TONY BURNS	VIC ANDRETTI
STUNNING LIGHTWEIGHT "POWERFUL"	HOXTON
BETHNAL GREEN	51 KO'S UNSTOPPABLE
V	V
BILLY "KNUCKLE" RUSHMOOR	BRIAN BRAZIER
SADLY KILLED HIS LAST OPPONENT	FEARLESS TOP FIGHTER
BROADMOOR	CROYDON
SCHEDULED FOR 6 X 3 MIN. ROUNDS	10 X 3 MIN. ROUNDS AT LIGHTWEIGHT "DON'T MISS"

Prices £1,00/- RINGSIDE £15/- OUTER RINGSIDE BALCONY. TEN BOB STANDING. HALF CROWN

TICKETS GEP TEX240 2123041   MAJOR BOXERS DIRECT- BOX 2300   ALL SPORTING OUTLETS

The Kray Twins Ronnie Kray & Reggie Kray Hand Written Letters

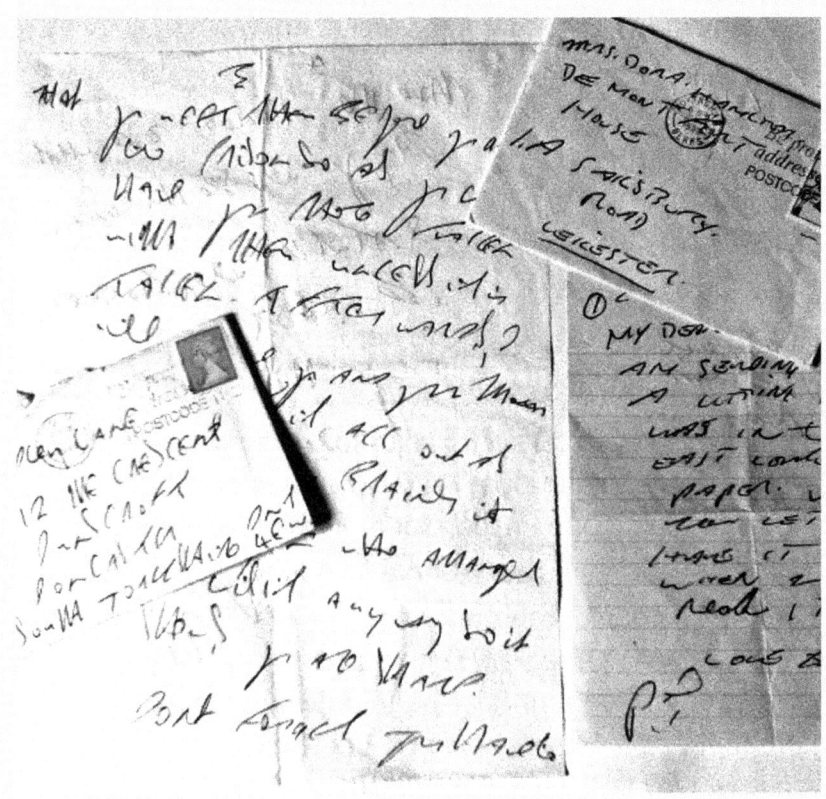

Frances Shea. the wife of gangster Reg Kray, was "wild child" who stood up to her fearsome husband and outshone celebs like Judy Garland at the Krays' nightclub, according to her niece Frances Shea

Dressed like an East End movie star, Frances Shea looked every inch the glamorous gangster's moll.

Yet history has cast Reggie Kray's wife as a timid victim who was bullied by the twins and committed suicide to escape.

That view is reinforced by the new film Legend which stars Tom Hardy as both Reggie and Ronnie Kray.

It portrays Frances - Franie to her family - as a "ghost" long before she took a fatal overdose in 1967.

There have even been claims of foul play with armed robber Bradley Allardyce, who became Reggie's gay lover in Maidstone Prison, claiming the infamous gangster told him that Ronnie killed Franie because he was jealous of their marriage.

And a new documentary suggests the Kray's mum Violet and their aunt Rose had Franie killed while pregnant because they didn't think she was fit to be a mother.

But according to her niece and namesake Frances Shea, Franie, far from being a timid wife was was a drug taking "wild child" who stood up to husband and outshone Judy Garland and Barbara Windsor at the Krays' nightclub.

Angry about the way Franie was portrayed in the film, Frances has spoken out to set the record straight.
She said: "I want people to laugh when they remember Franie, not cry.
"She was a vivacious, curvy woman, not the scrawny, scruffy girl we saw on that screen. She was a real wild child.
"When she jumped off the plane in Spain the first thing she asked for was hashish. That was our Franie."
Franie met Reggie Kray when she was just 16 years old and he was 10 years older.

They married in 1965 in a blaze of publicity but while Franie dazzled in a figure hugging white dress, her mother Elsie showed her disdain for the Krays by wearing black.
The marriage was tempestuous and Franie walked out for the first time just weeks after the wedding, before attempting to end her life several times as she battled withmental illness.
She even planned to shoot herself with a starting pistol that was hidden under her bed.
Before she died she wrote that she wanted her maiden name Frances Shea on her gravestone, but Reggie ensured she was buried as a Kray in the family plot in Chingford cemetery.

Wild: Reggie Kray's wife Frances Shea who committed suicide

The letters between Ronnie Kray and Lord Boothby have recently emerged

AD. 4466   Feb: 19th 65

House of Lords

Dear Mr. & Mrs. Kray,

sorry I did not write before. — I was asked by Lord Boothby to thank you for your kind wishes on his birthday. I do hope you are both well and not worrying too much. I am sure lots of people like myself realise the unfairness of this treatment of the twins. — Let's hope all will be well in the end.

regards to
Charlies
girls

Best wishes.
Sincerely,
Gwen Cuddlof

Breaks 50-year silence

The family of a man murdered by Ronnie Kray in the Blind Beggar pub have broken their 50-year silence over the killing.

George Cornell's son Billy has told how his dad's shooting at the East End boozer wrecked his family and has haunted him and younger sister Rayner ever since.

Billy, 58, says: "The Krays widowed my mother and orphaned two children, and my daughter and nieces and nephews never met their grandfather. My father was not the only victim that night.

"I hate the Krays and anyone who is part of their family – and worse, the people who hero-worship them today as some kind of glamorous Robin Hoods of the East End. They were vicious and evil."

The slaying of his father, which has been re-enacted countless times in films about the Kray twins – most recently in Legend, starring Tom Hardy – is one of Britain's most famous murders.

It illustrated the power the Krays believed they had, and demonstrated psychopath Ronnie's warped thirst for violence.

But it also signalled the beginning of the end of the twins' violent stranglehold over the East End of London.

Ronnie Kray was jailed for life for the killing and died behind bars.

His brother Reggie, who went on to kill Jack "The Hat" McVitie in Stoke Newington, North London, also got life for that murder.

George Cornell had known the Krays since childhood, when the three of them were growing up on the streets around Whitechapel, and for a time they even did business together.

George worked as a Billingsgate fish porter from the age of 12, and then at the nearby docks where he ran credit rackets.

Billy says: "Dad knew all the traders in Mile End and the guvnors of all the pubs. He made his money setting up warehouses and buying in goods on credit then selling them cheap and folding the business without paying his bills.

"He was from a very poor family but was physically strong and good with his fists. When people saw he could fight he got respect, they were afraid to challenge him.

Billy tells how, aged four, he went to the Krays' East London home with his dad for a business meeting.

He says: "I recall being in the front room and them drinking tea.

"Ronnie was very edgy, like he could snap at any point and his brother was flash with a nice suit and slick way about him."

He says his father grew to despise Ronnie in particular, and refused to show deference to the twins. He says: "Ronnie was gay and liked being with young boys and to my dad, who was a gentleman who wouldn't let anyone swear in front of a woman, in those days that was unacceptable."

Cornell left the East End in the mid-1950s when he married wife Olive from Camberwell, South London, and set up his family in two flats there.

Billy says: "He made a success of himself in the most difficult circumstances. He was always well turned out in Aquascutum suits, Burberry raincoats and crocodile skin shoes.

"We had money and nice food at Christmas and he had a car and we lived in two flats in south London and had a house in the countryside."

George became close to the Krays' arch rivals, South London's notorious Richardson gang – who, with their enforcer "Mad" Frankie Fraser terrorised London in the 1960s and 1970s.

And Cornell could look after himself. "Dad wasn't scared of anyone," says Billy. "I recall more than one occasion where he came home bashed up after a fight.

"One time we were in Maidstone, where we had a bungalow, and we'd stopped in the town centre so mum could get some cakes

"My dad parked his Austin 11, and we were waiting in the car when a bloke came over and told him not to park where he had as it was for cabs.

"My dad told him to 'leave off' and said he was only waiting for his wife but the bloke wouldn't let it go and three other men came over and were getting on to dad.

"He got out of the car and took all four of them on and gave them a hiding."

But it was Cornell's refusal to show fear to Ronnie Kray that was to sign his death warrant.

On March 8 1966 there was a bloody confrontation between the Kray gang and the Richardson gang at Mr Smiths nightclub in Catford, South London.

Richard Hart, a friend of Ronnie and Reggie , was shot dead outside the back doors. But the next day George Cornell went to the Krays' territory in the East End with two associates to visit a shot pal being treated at the Royal London Hospital.

Billy says: "My dad went into the Blind Beggar opposite the hospital for a pint after he had seen his mate.

"I'd seen him earlier that evening as I'd been a naughty boy and he'd given me a clip around the ear and sent me to bed. Dad was talking to someone he knew in the pub but they said they had to go – I think West Ham had just qualified for Europe and the only place you could get coverage was on the radio and he said he was going to listen to that.

"He didn't though, he went outside and called the Krays and told them dad was in the pub."

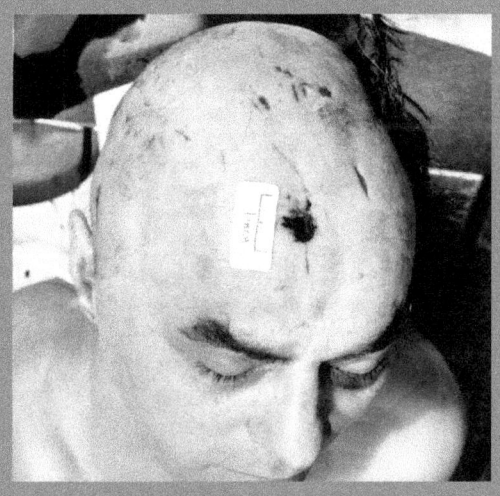

Blind Beggar after George was shot

Blood stains on the floor inside the Blind Beggar public house in Whitechapel where George Cornell was killed.

The Kray twins drove to the pub, stopping to pick up a gun on the way.

Billy says: "Dad was drinking and turned as the door opened and saw Ronnie, and said: 'Look what the cat's dragged in.'

"Ronnie pulled out a gun and as dad went to get off his stool he shot him in the head."

Legend has it that the juke box in the pub was playing the Walker Brothers song The Sun Ain't Going to Shine Anymore and a warning bullet which ricocheted off the ceiling made the record stick, playing the chorus over and over again.

Billy says: "I think dad probably knew what was coming when Ronnie walked in but he wasn't afraid of anyone. The twins drove off and my father was taken to the hospital but although they tried to save him he died two hours later.

"The two men he was with had to leave London as they knew they would be next as witnesses."

Back at the Cornell family home, young Billy was woken by the sound of his mum answering the telephone.

He says: "I could hear her saying 'who is this? What is your name?'

"She put down the phone and called my auntie Pat and told her a fella had phoned up and said dad had been shot.

"I must have gone back to sleep but when I woke up a couple of hours later and went into the lounge it was full of men sat smoking

"People were talking to me, asking me about football and how I was, but no one said dad was dead – but I knew he wasn't coming back again.

"It was mum who told me, she said: 'Your dad went out and there was a fight, it was with someone he has been angry with for a while, someone he worked with, he got killed.'

"It didn't really sink in, I don't know when it did. I know there was a big funeral and I wasn't allowed to go. I remember looking out the window of our flat at the square of green outside and it being covered in bunches of flowers, like a carpet.

"My father was liked and respected and people showed their respect."

But that was the end of the life young Billy had known. His mother, widowed in her 20s with a son of seven and six-month-old baby daughter, "never recovered", he says. She died from cancer aged 59, 20 years ago.

He says: "She loved dad from the moment they met to the day she died, she never got over his death."

In the hours after George died, Olive is said to have gone to the Krays' family home in Bethnal Green and thrown a brick through the front window.

He says: "She hated them more than anything in the world from the day he died."

Former market trader Billy, who now lives in Bermondsey, South London, fell into crime and was jailed for pick-pocketing several times.

He once served a 14-month term in Camp Hill Prison on the Isle of Wight, next door to Parkhurst Prison – home at the time to Ronnie Kray.

He says: "Mother begged me not to do anything if I ever saw him.

Billy hates the Kray twins

George Cornell and Olive at their 1950s wedding

Lightning Source UK Ltd.
Milton Keynes UK
UKHW01f1820070918
328516UK00012B/739/P